MW00881650

Praise for DEAD WOOD

"As gritty as the Detroit streets where it's set, DEAD WOOD grabs you early on and doesn't let go. As fine a a debut as you'll come across this year, maybe any year."
—*Tom Schreck*

"From its opening lines, Dan Ames and his private eye novel DEAD WOOD recall early James Ellroy: a fresh attitude and voice and the heady rush of boundless yearning and ambition. Ames delivers a vivid evocation of time and place in a way that few debut authors achieve, nailing the essence of his chosen corner of high-tone Michigan. This is the first new private eye novel in a long time that just swept me along for the ride. Ames is definitely one to watch."
—*Craig McDonald, Edgar-nominated author*

"Dead Wood is a fast-paced, unpredictable mystery with an engaging narrator and a rich cast of original supporting characters."
—*Thomas Perry, Edgar-winning author*

Dan Ames' writing reminds me of the great thriller writers -- lean, mean, no nonsense prose that gets straight to the point and keeps you turning those pages."
—*Robert Gregory Browne*

DEAD WOOD

BY DAN AMES

Hard Rock
Death by Sarcasm
Murder with Sarcastic Intent
Gross Sarcastic Homicide
The Killing League
The Murder Store
To Find a Mountain
The Circuit Rider
Killer's Draw
Beer Money
Killing the Rat
The Recruiter
Head Shot
Dr. Slick
Choke

DEAD WOOD

(A John Rockne Mystery)

by

Dan Ames

Copyright © 2015 by Dan Ames

We all need someone we can bleed on . . .
—The Rolling Stones

DEAD WOOD

One

It was New Year's Eve, and I was living my dream. I was a cop. The youngest guy on the force, pulling the worst of the shifts . . . but I couldn't have been happier.

I'd wanted to be a cop all my life.

It was a brutally cold New Year's Eve in Grosse Pointe, especially along the lake. A nasty Canadian wind was howling down and blasting Detroit with the kind of cold that ignores your clothes and tears directly into your skin.

I'd been a cop for six months. Just long enough to be taken off probation. Not long enough to be considered anything but a green rookie. I was in my squad car, driving down Lake Shore, thinking about the New Year's Eve party ahead, about how my girlfriend and I were going to celebrate.

Elizabeth Pierce was actually more than my girlfriend: she was my fiancée and a true Grosse Pointe blue blood. I was definitely marrying up.

I headed down Lake Shore Drive toward the Detroit border. I passed a house with three ten-foot angels on the roof. Thousands of Christmas lights lit up the house and yard, turning the quarter acre lot into a Las Vegas outpost. Across the street, the surprisingly vast, dark waters of Lake

St. Clair stood in stark contrast to the hundred thousand watts supplied by the Detroit Energy Company.

I turned right on Oxford, away from the lake, just as my radio broke the monotony of the wind's fury. I glanced at the dashboard clock. It read 11:18 p.m. It was listed as a 10-107. Possible intoxicated person. I jotted down the address and pressed the accelerator.

It would be my last call for the night. By the time I got back to the office, turned in the car, and did the paperwork, it would already be past midnight, probably closer to one a.m.

An image of Elizabeth floated through my mind. She would have her blond hair tied back tonight, her diamond earrings sparkling, a glass of champagne ready for me. She might even be a little drunk. We'd hang out, go to a couple of parties, then retire back to my place and ring in the New Year the best way of all.

I cruised up Oxford Street and flashed the spotlight on the street numbers until I came to 1370. I called in to dispatch, got out of the cruiser, and walked to the front door. The wind wasn't letting up farther from the lake. The sweat from my hand momentarily froze on the brass knocker and stung when I broke my hand free. I banged the knocker against the oak a few times, noticing the small, worn indentations where the metal had been knocked raw. An elderly woman in a glittery blouse with a cigarette between her fingers opened the door.

"He was staggering down the street," she said, gesturing with a shaking hand toward the other end of the street. The cigarette's red, glowing end bobbed in the dark with each tremor of her hand.

I could smell her breath, a strong dose of stale smoke. She was ancient, probably between eighty or ninety, with saggy skin and deep creases everywhere.

"How long ago?" I said.

"Just a few minutes. The poor boy was going to freeze to death. He wasn't wearing a shirt even. These kids." She shook her head. "Sometimes they act like animals!" Her voice was raspy and thick. She ran her tongue over her lips.

"Can you describe him?"

"Thin. Pale. Young." She squinted at me through the cigarette smoke. "Younger than you."

"Which way did he go?"

She nodded with her head. "He's probably still staggering around. Look under a shrub or two, you'll find him." Her little laugh sounded like a cat coughing up a hairball.

"Thanks for the advice, ma'am. Have a good New Year."

I turned before I could hear her response. Back in the squad car, I called in to dispatch again and put the car in gear, then prowled slowly up the block. The homes were alive with lights and colors, glimpses of holiday sweaters, hands clutching eggnog cups or champagne glasses. The twinkle of trees decorated with Christmas lights sparkled through the big picture windows.

On the second block down, I saw him.

A smear of white skin in the night. I pulled the squad car up next to the kid, radioed dispatch, then parked and got out.

"How you doin' tonight?" I said, pointing the flashlight in the kid's face. Young. Maybe around eighteen, I figured. Big brown eyes, his hair wild, his shirt gone, in jeans and barefoot. I didn't see any signs of frostbite, but he couldn't be out in this cold much longer. His skin was nearly purple.

The kid looked at me, but recognition was dim. He mumbled something, but it was incoherent. Not a single identifiable word escaped his lips. I could smell the booze, though. Strong. Almost fruity. Like peach schnapps or something.

"Sending the year out in style, are we?" I asked. "There must be a helluva party somewhere."

The kid mumbled something and tried to walk away. I grabbed his arm and he sagged. I knew what I had to do. Put him in the back of the squad car, book him for public drunkenness, and let him dry out in jail. Shitty way to kick off the New Year.

I helped him to his feet, planned to take him to the car and into the station, when the man appeared from around the corner.

"Ah, Officer!" the man called. I turned. He was bundled up in a thick winter jacket, and he had a wool fedora, the kind with the built-in ear flaps, pulled down. At first, I thought he was a woman from the way he ran. His hips moved with a swishing motion. His thick, black glasses were nearly steamed up with the melted snow glistening on the lenses. He was a little older than the kid, probably in his mid to late twenties. But it was hard to tell.

"Oh my God, Benjamin," the man said, producing a leather coat, which he helped onto the boy. His voice was high and wavering with a thick lisp. "This is my responsibility, Officer, not Ben's. This should never have happened." He shook his head like a disappointed mother. "He had an office Christmas party today, and then he was hitting the cocktails when I left to get thyme for the chicken, and when I came back, he was gone. I've been going crazy trying to find him."

"Could I see some identification, sir?" I said.

The man, wearing gloves, gently withdrew a wallet from his back pocket. I looked at the address on the license as the man zipped up the coat he'd put on the boy. The address was just a few blocks over. I glanced at the picture and the name on the license. The picture matched.

I handed the license back to the man and studied the kid once more. "Benjamin, what's your last name?" I shone the flashlight in the kid's eyes. He didn't wince or look away.

"Collins, Officer," the man said. "His name is Benjamin Collins. I'm so sorry about this, sir," the man continued, his voice high and nervous. I stepped back to the cruiser, called dispatch, and had them run Benjamin Collins through the system. The name came back clean. I had dispatch run the man through the system too. He came back without any hits.

I thought about it. The kid was in bad shape. By the time he was booked, printed, and in an actual jail cell, he'd be even worse. I thought about one time in high school when a cop pulled me over. I had a beer between my legs and a twelve-pack in the trunk. He made me dump everything out and go home, rather than taking me in, calling my parents, and basically ruining my life. That act of kindness was a better lesson than being thrown into a holding cell with a bunch of lowlifes.

Well, I thought, *now's my chance to return the favor.* Besides, it was New Year's Eve. Who wanted to start the year off in jail?

I walked back to find the man slipping winter boots onto the kid's feet. "Okay," I said. "Get him home. I'll give him a warning this time, but if I ever see his name come up again . . ."

"Perfectly understood, Officer," the man said. He shook my hand heartily. "Again, I'm so sorry. He's a beautiful, beautiful person, but when he drinks, sometimes . . ."

He put his arm around the boy and began walking away, practically carrying the younger man. The wind had picked up and was now packing a ferocious wallop.

"Want a lift?" I asked.

"That's quite all right, Officer." The man's voice was nearly lost in the wind. "We're right around the corner."

I watched them turn the corner, then got back in the car and wiped the snow from my face. I called in my position.

In my mind, I had done my final good deed of the year. In my mind, I had finished out the New Year the best way possible, doing something nice for someone, and now it was time to see a beautiful girl about a glass of champagne.

•

The call came at five twenty-one in the morning. About an hour past mine and Elizabeth's final lovemaking session of the night.

I untangled my body from Elizabeth's and listened to the voice of Chief Michalski telling me to get down to the Yacht Club immediately.

Fifteen minutes later, I watched as Benjamin Collins' body was loaded into the coroner's van. They'd found his ID on the frozen pier just twenty feet or so from where his nude, mutilated body had been seen bobbing in the small patch of water heated by the Yacht Club's boiler runoff.

I stood there in the cold, as numb and unfeeling as I'd ever been in my entire life. They let me look at the body. It was a sight I would never forget.

By the end of the day, I'd given my version of the events of the night before well over a dozen times. To the chief. To internal investigators. I desperately wanted to join in the search for the man to whom I'd turned over Benjamin Collins, but I was kept away from the investigation. Left to sit in a room and think about what I'd done.

No one had chewed me out. No one blamed me for fucking up, but it was there just the same.

Finally, the chief called me in and asked for my gun and badge. It was administrative leave. Until things were sorted out and the killer was caught. Until then, I was gone. The department might be liable should Collins' relatives seek litigation. I left his office, taking one last look at my gun and badge before he swept them off his desk and into his drawer.

I never got them back.

Two

Six Years Later

The gloved fist smashed through the glass of the shop's back door. The impact as well as the sound of shards tinkling to the floor went unnoticed by the workshop's sole occupant. The woman at the large workbench heard only the high-pitched buzz of the random orbit sander.

Nor did she hear the sound of the deadbolt thrown back, the doorknob turning, and the heavy door swinging open.

The only noise to reach her ears was that of the sander as its 220-grit sandpaper gently bit into the five-hundred-year-old wood. She moved the sander along the wood's surface with confident precision. Her honey-colored hair was tied back in a ponytail. Thick shop glasses distorted the Lake Michigan blue of her eyes as the powdery sawdust flying from the sander coated her hands and covered her hair like a thin veil.

The woman leaned back from the workbench and flicked off the sander. As the whine of the motor instantly began to descend, she brushed the layer of dust from the wood. Even through the gauze of the powder, the beauty of the grain was apparent. This had been a special batch:

ancient elm, filled with grain patterns and whorls that would be breathtaking after a light stain and varnish were applied.

She leaned back and studied the beginning stage of the guitar. It was to be a semi-acoustic twelve-string, made from centuries-old elm salvaged from the bottom of Lake Michigan. It was for a rocker in California, who had paid her the first half of the price tag: five thousand dollars. She was taking her time with this one, especially after the monumental task she'd just accomplished.

She glanced over at the finished guitar in question. A jumbo acoustic, her most ambitious and most expensive guitar yet. Made from the rarest, most expensive woods of all: virgin tiger maple, hickory, ash, and ebony. All of it salvaged from the bottom of Lake Michigan. All of it priceless. All of it breathtakingly, stunningly beautiful. And she had used all of her skills, all of her powers to turn those woods into a guitar. A guitar with a sound so rich and so pure you almost forgot how beautiful it looked.

And it already had a buyer.

Jesse brushed her hands off on her jeans and went to the guitar. She picked it up and felt the perfect weight of it.

She sat back on her stool and strummed the strings, the full beauty of the sound echoing in the shop's interior. Her fingers naturally picked out a melancholy melody, and she played quietly, confidently.

Her mind ran free, loosened by the change from the one-note orbit sander to this instrument of the gods.

As she played, she thought about how she enjoyed every aspect of building guitars. From the beginning design stages, to selecting the raw materials, to the painstaking construction, and all the way through the finishing touches. Each instrument was a unique endeavor, with its own moments of sheer beauty.

At the thought of her craft, a sense of sadness rose within her. The guitar on her table would be the last one she would build for quite some time.

A new chapter was beginning, one that in the deepest, most secret part of her heart, she'd dreamed would one day come true.

Her fingers finished playing the tune with a strong downstroke, and the chord reverberated, its beautiful sound echoing through the shop.

And then she heard the gentle sound of a foot scraping the ground behind her. She turned, peering into the darkness.

The man charged at her with astonishing speed. She got no more than a quick glimpse of his face—a face she may have seen before. His hands were raised over his head. She had just enough time to recognize the heavy hammer she sometimes used to tap a chisel along the rough edges of a plank of wood. It was in his hands, raised high, coming toward her.

She ducked her head, and then, in the final act of her life, she put her arms around the guitar and leaned over it, trying to protect it.

Jesse Barre never felt the crushing blow that caved in her skull and drove her from her stool onto the floor.

Her blood pooled on the concrete, the flakes of sawdust soaking up the crimson liquid.

The guitar remained safe, still cradled in her arms.

Three

"So here's the hook," Nate said.

We were in a booth at the Village Grill, a little Greek diner smack dab in the middle of Grosse Pointe proper. It had big, overstuffed booths, low lighting conditions, and a bar with a brass rail and a big-screen TV. The perfect lunch spot for two guys who thought arugula was an island somewhere near the Caribbean.

Nate Becker was the only full-time reporter for the *Grosse Pointe Times* and a friend from way back. We'd known each other since he was a chubby little kid who got picked on all the time and I was his defender. Unless the wind happened to be blowing the other way and I was one of the kids picking on him. You know how kids are. We were no different.

Now we were both grownups, sort of, and he was doing a piece on me, John Rockne, Grosse Pointe's very own private investigator. It was part of a monthly feature on local businesses. Last week it was the lady caterer whose van was decorated like a giant swordfish.

Prestigious company indeed.

I hadn't really done anything to deserve the attention, but the business district of Grosse Pointe isn't very big—sooner or later, it's just your turn.

"Hook?" I said.

"Yeah, you know, the angle of the story. The unique approach that intrigues the reader."

"What was your hook for the swordfish lady?"

"I didn't need one for her. She was interesting."

"Thanks," I said. "So let's hear it."

Nate spread his hands like he was serving me a platter of caviar. "You're the PI who doesn't just fight crime, you fight clichés," he said.

I rolled my eyes and signaled the waitress. She came over, a cute girl in her twenties wearing the unfortunate decision of a pierced tongue. I made a mental note to floss after lunch. I ordered two Cokes. Diet for me, regular for Nate.

"What?" he said. "It's a perfect hook."

I recognized the look in Nate's eye. It meant he had just gotten in a fresh load of bullshit, and he needed to spew.

"Cliché fighter?" I said.

He nodded as the waitress set our Cokes down on the table. "You're not some shady bum with a checkered past," he said. "A half-criminal who has more in common with the thugs he chases than he does with the rest of us on the right side of the law."

"Jesus Christ, you're full of it," I said.

"Work with me, dumb ass," he said. "You went to college, got a degree in criminology . . ."

". . . and a minor in psychology. . ."

". . . worked as a cop to learn the ropes, then worked for a big PI firm before getting your own license."

I actually appreciated Nate's effort. Most of it was true. The problem was he had conveniently edited out a certain bad spot in my career. For Nate, the problem was twofold. One, I was his friend, and he didn't want to dredge up bad memories. And two, the story had been told already. Many, many times.

So Nate would skip it altogether. I guess that's the beauty of editing.

"You don't carry a gun," he said. He was on a roll, and I didn't want to stop him.

"Just a Nikon."

"You're definitely not a tall, dark, and handsome, Mickey Spillane-type ladies man."

I just shook my head at that one. "You've got a real nose for the truth," I said.

"What?" he said. "You didn't get your hands on a pair of tits until the dairy farm field trip our senior year of high school."

He had a point there, the bastard.

"The fact that you're married is less about you and more about the unceasing generosity of women."

"Glad you're not pulling any punches," I said. "I think I'll go back to my office and hang myself."

Our food arrived. A turkey on rye for me. A Double Boss Burger with an extra large order of fries for Nate. Food was his way to deal with stress. Three years ago, his first child, a boy, had been born without a pulmonary artery. A small oversight on the ultrasound technician's part. After many operations, the little guy was doing fine, but there was still a certain amount of concern about him. Nate, at five feet eight inches, had always been a little chunky. Now he weighed nearly three hundred fifty pounds.

"Plus, you're not some lone wolf, like PIs are supposed to be," he continued. "You know, the guy haunted by some lost love, or grieving over the unfortunate death of his young wife. You're a family man with two young girls." Nate doused his fries with salt and took a huge bite from his Boss Burger.

"And don't forget," I said. "No one's firebombed my house or framed me as a presidential assassin."

Nate nodded. He knew everything there was to know about me. This interview was really just an excuse to get together for lunch, which we do every week anyway, but because of the story, it was being paid for by the paper.

"Here's a thought," I said. "This may sound kind of crazy—but do you think you can actually work in a few positive things—you know, stuff that might actually be good for business?"

"Won't that be false advertising?" he said through a mouth full of fries.

"Good point," I said. "Stick with your 'ugly and dull' angle. Customers will be beating down my door."

"The truth shall set you free," he said.

"Okay, I like the whole 'Average Joe' approach," I said. "As long as you don't make me sound like I'm light in the loafers."

"So you want me to lie."

"I'm just a normal guy trying to do a good job for his customers. I'm fair, honest, and reliable."

"Fucking boring as a box of rocks," Nate said.

I was going to give him a shot back, but he'd already tucked into the Boss Burger. I knew that he was so into his meal there was no doubt about whether or not he was listening. It didn't matter. He'd do a good story on me.

And since the paper was buying, I ordered another Diet Coke.

Cliché fighter, my ass.

Four

He stood outside my office door, a tall, broad-shouldered figure in faded blue jeans, a colorful shirt, black leather vest, and shiny, black cowboy boots. His powder-white hair was thick and combed straight back. The eyes beneath the white brows were blazing blue and unclouded, twin shafts of cool set on a lined, weathered face. But there was more than just age on his face. More than fatigue as well. It was something I'd seen only a few times in my life—but once you see it, you remember.

"Can I help you?" I asked, the keys to my office in hand. I felt tired and full from lunch. I don't know if it was because of Nate's eating problem or what, but I always ate more when I was with him. Or at least that was my excuse and I was sticking with it.

"Are you John Rockne?" Marshal Dillon asked. His voice had a deep gravel to it—whiskey and cigarettes and two a.m. closing calls.

"Guilty as charged," I said, stifling a belch. I unlocked the door and let him into my office. "How can I help you?"

He took a brief look around and then turned and faced me. He held out his hand and I took it. "Clarence Barre," he said. "You're the private investigator?"

I gestured toward the door, which read Grosse Pointe Investigations. "Like the sign says . . ."

24

An uneasy smile crossed his face. Most clients had the same look. It was part shame, part anger, part fear. Going to see a PI wasn't much different than going to a shrink for most people. It was all about letting a complete stranger into their personal lives. And in most cases, the deepest, ugliest part of their personal lives. Not an easy thing to do, for anyone.

My office was on the second floor of a small brick building built in 1927. The ground floor was a jewelry store that I went into once a few years back, thinking I might buy my wife a necklace. I soon realized that asking her to sign the paperwork for a second and third mortgage would spoil the surprise. I haven't been back since.

My office consisted of a small waiting room, complete with two chairs and a table. The chairs are from the fifties, the table the seventies, and the carpeting's genealogy is too hard to trace. I'd say it was coming off the textile rolls right around the time Jackie was scrambling off the back of the big Lincoln in Dallas.

There were a few framed paintings of sailboats on the walls, even though I'm not a big fan of the water, as I already mentioned. A lot of clients seem to expect pictures of sailboats from a Grosse Pointe PI. Sometimes people are reassured by the cliché, and I don't like to disappoint prospective clients.

The place reeked of coffee. To me, it was a great smell, especially on a cold winter day. I always had a pot brewing. Nate would probably not put that into the article, because it is a bit of a cliché. But hey, I fucking liked coffee . . . damn them if a bunch of other PIs did too.

On the table were magazines. *Police Times*, *Small Firearms Journal*, *S.W.A.T. Illustrated*. I wanted my clients to feel confident in my ability. Somehow, six months worth of *Martha Stewart Living* might make them think twice about hiring me.

I went around behind my desk, a small oak number that weighed about five hundred pounds. A laptop computer, a phone, and a stack of files sat on top.

"Have we met?" I asked. "You seem familiar."

He just looked at me and then from deep within him came a baritone hum. It changed pitch and soon a short melody became apparent.

"Get the fuck out of here," I said. I knew that tune, and I knew that voice.

"Mississippi Honey?"

He nodded. "That's right. Clarence Barre, country singer/songwriter."

I loved that song. Actually, it was a bit of a source of embarrassment. I'd finally gotten a girl into the backseat of my car in high school. "Mississippi Honey" was in the tape deck, playing along as I'd gotten Tracy Woeburg's pants down and then had absolutely no idea what I was supposed to do next.

In the middle of my reverie, I realized my potential client was staring at me. I caught myself, felt kind of foolish about what he may have seen play across my face.

"Don't worry," he said. "That happens all the time. I consider it a compliment. That my song evokes . . . memories."

He smiled then. A sad, weary gesture. And suddenly, it came to me where else I remembered the name. I knew Clarence Barre because he had been a relatively well-known musician for a brief period in the seventies. He was from Detroit, and after his career, he'd moved back to Grosse Pointe.

So I knew the name Barre. Had heard it recently.

But not a man. Not Clarence. The recognition must have shown on my face because the small smile that had lingered on his face now vanished.

Whatever stupid thing I was going to say got stuck in my mouth. Clarence rushed to fill the pause.

"I'm here about my daughter," he said. "Jesse." Suddenly, all of the color in his face seemed to vanish, draw back in on itself and pool in his eyes. They smoldered, two pools of blazing blue.

Now it was my turn to nod. The killing had been big news in Grosse Pointe. Probably for two reasons: one, there weren't a lot of murders in Grosse Pointe. And two, Jesse Barre had been a very beautiful young woman. A guitar maker, I remembered.

"She was killed during a robbery, as I recall," I answered.

"You're half right," he said.

The look on my face was a question.

"She was killed. But it wasn't a robbery. Someone wanted her dead."

Oh boy, I thought.

"Is that what the police think?" I said.

He shook his head. "It's what I *know*."

"You want me to find out who killed her?"

"Nope," he said. "I already know who did it."

My face was again an open question.

"I just want you to help me prove it."

Five

"His name is Nevada Hornsby," Clarence Barre said. He spoke slowly and softly. Enunciating carefully. Not out of respect, but because his emotions were running so strong it took every effort not to insert an expletive.

I had a million questions: did the police know? If not, why wasn't he talking to them? How did he know Hornsby killed her?

As much as I wanted to ask, I decided to wait Mr. Barre out. He'd just lost his daughter. I thought he deserved a chance to explain himself.

"I told Jesse time and time again not to get involved with him," he said. "She wouldn't listen. In fact, she told me to back off. So I did. And look where it got us."

He paused again.

Just when I was about to start the questions, he said, "The cops don't think he did it. They say he has an alibi. Well, of course he does! Who the fuck couldn't come up with an alibi? Only the stupidest of criminals can't come up with a friggin' alibi, for God's sake. So they're believing his bullshit, but see, they don't know him. I do."

His voice had grown in intensity. And this was a man who had used his voice to great effect for many years. It didn't fail him now.

"Okay," I said.

He fixed his eyes on me, willing me to understand. I leaned in toward him, hoping to give him the nudge he needed to tell me just what the hell he was getting at.

"He's an ex-con."

"Okay," I said. I got out a notepad and pen. "Do you know what he was in for?"

"I'm sure it was something bad. Assault. I remember Jesse saying something about a fight. She claimed he hadn't started it. Christ, he had her hook, line, and sinker."

"Do you have a reason to doubt his alibi?"

"I met him," he said.

I wrote the word "NO" down on my notepad and underlined it.

"I know all about men like that. They don't value life. Prison teaches them to look at everything differently. Jesse didn't realize that. She was overly sympathetic. That's how I would put it. Wanting to prove that she respected people for who they are, not who they've been."

He ran a hand through the thick, white hair. It reminded me of Kenny Rogers' hair. I wrote down "Kenny Rogers" on my notepad. Goofy, I know, but it was amazing sometimes the things that jogged the memory. Who knew, maybe a year from now I'd be looking at my notes on the Barre case, see the Kenny Rogers reference and have some brilliant flash of insight.

I looked at Clarence Barre. Goddamn, I found myself liking him. He had a great face, wide open and honest. I could sense the goodness in him. The pain of losing a loved one.

But I wasn't going to take a case just because a father was having difficulty dealing with the loss of a child. He probably hated this Hornsby guy and made him into a convenient target for his anger and loss. If the police had checked out the alibi and crossed him off the list, he was probably innocent.

I wasn't going to take the case. No way. To take Mr. Barre's money would be another crime.

He must have seen the look on my face because he said, "I know how this must look. A guy just pointing a finger and saying, 'He did it.'"

That's exactly how it looked to me.

"How long were your daughter and this Hornsby seeing each other?"

"Way too long."

"Can you be more specific?"

"Years."

"Had there been any sign of physical abuse? Any problems? Fights?"

"No, but Jesse and I hadn't seen each other on a regular basis," he said. And now I could hear even more, deeper pain in his voice. The loss of a loved one you'd fallen out with over petty differences. No getting them back now.

"But as far as you knew—"

"She didn't say anything, and no, I never saw any bruises or anything on her. But Jesse was very private. Believe me, if she'd wanted to hide something, it would stay hidden until she wanted you to find it."

"Did the police say if they have any other suspects?"

"I don't know. They aren't saying."

This was about as bogus as it got. Mr. Barre wanted me to make him feel better. He wanted me to make him feel like he was doing something for the daughter he'd grown apart from. Now, when it was too late, he was trying to make things right. I had no intention of taking his money.

I started to tell him that, but he cut me off.

"I just want you to keep an open mind about it and check it out. I'll pay whatever your rates are and your expenses. If you honestly find out Hornsby had nothing to do with it, and can give me some kind of proof, we'll shake hands and go our separate ways."

He pushed back a little and folded his arms across his chest.

I write on my notepad: no. No way. Nuh-uh.
I said, "I'll think about it."

•

When I was younger, I used to be very impatient. My dad tried to teach me how to make model airplanes, but I would race through, gluing all the parts together without waiting for them to dry. I would crack open the new box after breakfast and be done before lunch. My plane would always end up shoddily built with a sloppy paint job, and the little decals were always crooked. It might have been a few weeks later, or sometimes even a few months later, when my Dad would finish his. And naturally, it was the picture of perfection. It took quite a while, and quite a few botched P-47s, for me to realize the problem.

Now I sometimes had become the opposite, perhaps in reaction to what my impatient youth had taught me. I tended to wait and think things over. Maybe even over think them a bit. It was probably because I had children of my own, and if there's one thing a parent needs, it's patience.

So despite the fact that I had no intention of taking on the case, I decided to think it over. It seemed to me that Clarence Barre was dealing with the death of his daughter the only way he knew how. In his case, it happened to be blaming a man who was most likely innocent. Not something of which I really wanted to be a part. Even if it meant turning down a paycheck.

I also had to admit that I liked the earnest honesty of Clarence Barre. Maybe it was the way he looked me in the eye, or the obvious pain that hung on his weathered face.

Or maybe it was that damn Kenny Rogers hair.

Six

After Mr. Barre left my office, I logged onto the Internet and searched for newspaper accounts of Jesse Barre's murder. I found nothing in the local paper, but that didn't surprise me. The Grosse Pointe newspaper was legendary for not publicizing any stories of crime. Why? Because on the scale of priorities, Grosse Pointe residents placed property values on the same level as breathing. Perhaps even a nudge higher. A weekly report of all the petty crimes that occurred mostly on the direct border with Detroit, more frequently that most would like to admit, might make people think twice about plopping down a half million dollars on that picturesque Tudor with three fireplaces and an annual tax that could make a grown man choke on his bacon-wrapped filet mignon.

Anyway, I found what I was looking for on the *Detroit Free Press* website. The article there gave me the basic facts: the murder took place at Jessica Barre's studio on Kercheval, just a few blocks from the Detroit border. It was an abandoned shoe repair shop that she'd converted to a guitar-making studio. The murder took place at approximately eleven p.m. Forced entry. Blunt force trauma. DOA. The article said it appeared to be a robbery but didn't elaborate. The murder weapon, a heavy hammer that belonged to the victim, was left next to her body.

It was all very straightforward to me. Although Grosse Pointe was by and large a very safe community, when you spent that much time right on the border with Detroit, sometimes bad things could happen. On the Alter Road border, it was pretty common for bicycles and children's toys to be snatched from the yard. Patio furniture was even known to sometimes get up in the middle of the night and walk across the border into Detroit, never to be heard from again. Same goes for grills and portable basketball hoops.

The other street that bordered Detroit, Mack Avenue, was legendary for carjackings, purse snatchings, and even the occasional bank robbery.

Hey, when your neighbor was one of the most dangerous cities in the country, you had to expect it. Over the years, Grosse Pointe residents had become naturally inured to the bullshit, although on the few occasions something really bad happened, it often gave pause to consider a move to the northern suburbs where McMansions and golf courses rule the land.

I skimmed the *Free Press* article once again. It all seemed pretty clear cut to me. Someone had probably seen the guitars, a woman working alone, probably late at night. They broke in, killed her, and grabbed what they could. Leaving the murder weapon and wiping it free of prints indicated a certain sophistication, I had to admit, but for the most part, it was probably what it seemed: a robbery that had gotten rough. Innocent people in robberies were killed all the time. Fast-food workers killed execution-style in the walk-in freezer. Why? Because some cold, sadistic psycho didn't want any witnesses left alive. Or maybe a punk with a gun wanted to feel the ultimate power. Who knew?

There was only one thing that seemed to stick in the back of my brain as I re-read the article. It seemed odd to me that a thief, even taking into account the fact that not all thieves are terribly clever, would choose to knock over a guitar studio. It's not a cash business. It wasn't sexually motivated; at least there was no mention of an assault in the papers. And guitars would not be a terribly hot item on the market. From what I'd read and from the impression Clarence Barre had given me, the guitars Jesse Barre made were unique. I wasn't exactly an expert on robbery and the fencing of stolen goods, but it seemed that trying to sell a Jesse Barre guitar locally would likely present problems. It also held that most guitar stores would not only recognize one of Jesse's guitars, but would also have heard of the murder. My guess was that the cops had already called all the guitar stores and told them to be on the lookout for the kind of guitars she made. They would urge the shops to get a description and, if possible, a license plate of anyone trying to sell a Jesse Barre guitar. Pretty standard procedure.

I took a deep breath and thought some more. What if Clarence was right? What if this Hornsby had killed Jesse Barre and made it look like a robbery? That too was a trick as old as the hills. I suspected the cops had looked into it, Clarence said Hornsby had an alibi, but alibis can be manufactured. Good ones take a lot of time and effort and planning. Would this Hornsby, the ex-con, be able to do it?

I saved the article to my computer's desktop and pushed away from the desk, propping my feet on the low bookcase next to the wastebasket. I put my hands behind my head and thought about Clarence Barre. I knew that I liked him. And my wife has told me time and time again that I put a filter on my brain when it comes to people I like. That I see too much of the positive in people, sometimes even create it when it's not there. Maybe so. There was the off chance that I was looking for something that would justify my case for taking on Clarence Barre as a client.

But objectivity is a bastard. The fact was I knew the criminal mind was not a bastion of logic. Throw some booze and drugs into the mix and you've got a human being reduced to his or her most base instincts. A desperate person walks by a studio that may or may not be some kind of cash business, it's night, a woman is working alone on loud woodworking machines—the perfect opportunity for a smash-and-grab. Maybe the woman tries to defend herself or her products, and things get out of hand. It happens.

In fact, the more I thought about it, the more I thought Clarence Barre was most likely off base and wrapped up in the emotions of a grieving father, and that I had somehow fallen victim to his genuine earnestness.

My first impression of Clarence Barre was that he was a good man. Had probably been a good father. And he was a man who loved and cherished his daughter above all else, including logic. He was a good man, but he was probably wrong.

It seemed like there was really one right decision here.

But you know, I'd made so many fucking mistakes in my lifetime that one more couldn't hurt.

I would take the case.

Seven

London

The Spook was disappointed.

The investment banker's apartment was extremely luxurious. Marble floors. Turkish rugs. Original artwork worthy, in some cases, of museums.

All of which didn't surprise the Spook. After all, the banker had been skimming profits, stealing from the bank's partners for years. From the dossier that had been given to him, the Spook learned the investment banker had pilfered nearly twenty million dollars. The man's partners, some of whom had ties to various illegal activities themselves, were not happy. Undue attention in their business could prove to be lethal.

None of that disappointed or even interested the Spook. What upset him was the quality of the guitars. Surrounded by trappings of extreme wealth, the guitars were a joke. A run-of-the-mill Yamaha acoustic, a new Fender, and that was about it. Even worse, the guitars were dusty and out of tune. The strings hadn't been changed in ages. A disgrace.

The Spook was a guitar player. Although he loved his work, loved to get paid to kill people, he lived for music. The piercing wail of a bent third string, the soul-shaking shudder of a bluesy vibrato . . . it moved him in ways nothing else could. He looked at the guitars and shook his head.

This man deserved to die.

The Spook checked his watch. The banker's name was Gordon Springs, and the Spook knew from countless hours of surveillance that he was due home in ten minutes. A routine that the man never failed to repeat, day after day, month after month. The human need for structure made the Spook's job all that much easier.

He went to the nearest guitar, the Yamaha acoustic, and picked it up from its holder. Finding a pick and a slide—one couldn't very well perform intricate finger work wearing surgeon's gloves—he tuned the guitar to an open G and played a few notes. It didn't sound that great. The strings were very old, and there was a rattle near the bridge. To the Spook, it was how a social worker must feel to hold a neglected baby.

He made some adjustments then played the opening to "You Got the Silver" from Beggars Banquet. One of his idol's masterpieces of subtlety. No one could make a guitar do things the way Keith Richards could. Keith was more than just the famous guitarist of the infamous Rolling Stones, he was the Spook's god. The Spook felt that what he was to the profession of assassins, Keith was to the profession of rock and roll.

He finished off the song and set the guitar back in its stand. The guitar pissed off the Spook. To be here, in London, Keith Richards' home stomping grounds, and to see an apartment filled with expensive shit but mistreated guitars . . . well, it went against everything he believed in.

He checked his watch. Any minute now.

He went back to the guitar and turned the third string's tuning key until the string itself began to sag and hang away from the body of the guitar. The Spook continued unwinding until he could pull the string through the tuning key's hole, and then he popped the plastic peg that held the string in place at the center of the guitar's body. When it was free, he took two kitchen towels, placed them in the palm of his hand, and then wound an end of the string around each hand.

Moments later, he heard the key in the lock, and he disappeared into the darkness of the apartment. He heard the door swing open, a pause, and then the door clicked shut. He heard Mr. Springs sigh. Relief at living another day without falling off the tightrope that is the criminal life. The Spook knew Mr. Springs had a mistress, a drinking problem, and a severe lack of self-control, but he didn't care. Mr. Springs wasn't a person—he was simply an assignment.

The Spook listened as footsteps echoed on the hardwood floor. Then the footsteps stopped. The Spook knew exactly what the banker was doing.

He emerged from the shadows.

The banker stood in the kitchen, his back to the living room. The Spook had rented a flat directly across the street with a perfect view of Mr. Springs' apartment. Because of this, the Spook knew that Mr. Springs' answering machine was on the kitchen counter and that the first thing Mr. Springs did when he got home every evening was put his briefcase on the kitchen's island and then turn his full attention to the answering machine.

The Spook stood behind the British investment banker for just a moment, then reached up and looped the guitar string, cross-handed, over the man's head. Springs heaved back, but the Spook easily pivoted and brought him down, then kneeled on the man's back. He worked the thin metal cord back and forth like a saw until it had thoroughly cut through the soft flesh of the banker's neck. The Spook heard a scream reduced to soft gurgles. Springs thrashed for several seconds before his nerves received their final instructions.

And then Springs was dead.

His contract with the bank's partners fulfilled, the Spook stood, wiped the blood off the string with one of the kitchen towels, then went back to the guitar. He threaded the string back through the tuning key, tapped the peg back in place, and wound the string tight, tuning by ear.

The Spook picked up the glass slide and confidently eased into the opening licks of "Moonlight Mile."

He only had time for one or two songs.

The guitar sucked, sure. But his hero had played on worse.

This one definitely went out for Keith.

Eight

The address Clarence Barre had given me was on a street called Rivenoak, along the small strip of homes east of Jefferson. It was a valuable stretch of property, bordered on one side by Lake St. Clair. On the other side of Jefferson was the bulk of Grosse Pointe, acting as a thick layer of insulation from the depravity of Detroit proper.

The neighborhoods here were very upscale. Big lots, big houses, big money. The royalties from Clarence's backlist must have been both large and frequent.

The house itself was a statuesque colonial. It was between two larger Tudors and just a few houses in from Lake St. Clair. A small cul-de-sac with benches and wildflowers was at the end of the street. Clarence could stroll down here after dinner, smoke a cigar, and watch the boats pass by and the gulls doing their thing. He probably would have done something like that before his daughter's death. Now, my guess was that if he did come down and look out over the water, he'd think the kind of thoughts no parents should have to entertain. Someone once said the most painful thing in the world is to outlive your children. Seemed to me to be a pretty safe bet.

I parked my car, a utilitarian gray Taurus, in the stamped concrete driveway. I went to the door and used

40

the brass knocker, trying to tap out the bass line to Clarence's "Mississippi Honey."

He answered the door wearing the same kind of outfit he'd worn to my office: jeans, a colorful shirt, and a black leather vest. Shiny, pointed-toe cowboy boots as well. They looked to be of the same kind of leather as the bolo tie around his neck.

We shook hands, and then he showed me in to his living room. It was like the man himself—warm, rugged, and comfortable. Leather furniture, dark Persian rugs, some gold records on the wall as well as some pictures of a younger Clarence Barre with some minor and not-so-minor celebrities.

"Can I get you anything, Mr. Rockne?" he asked.

"Please, call me John. No thanks, I'm fine." We each took a leather club chair, and he looked at me questioningly.

"So . . ."

"What can you tell me about Nevada Hornsby?"

An almost imperceptible smile crossed Clarence's face. He knew I was taking the case. In fact, he'd probably known before I had.

"He runs a salvage operation out of St. Clair Shores," Clarence said.

"Salvage, like sunken ships?"

"Wood. Old lumber that sunk hundreds of years ago. It's valuable stuff. Jesse used it to make her guitars."

"So that's how they met," I said.

He nodded. "Ironically, in my mind, when she started using that salvaged lumber was when her career really took off. She'd tried different stuff, built a pretty big following with exotic woods. But when she started using the stuff from Hornsby, everything changed. For the better."

"Even her personal life," I added.

He didn't like that. "That's how she saw it, I'm sure. But I never liked the guy from day one. Real quiet. Standoffish. Like he had something to hide."

"Such as . . ."

"Who knows?"

I looked at my notes. "He's got an alibi."

"The alibi is bullshit," he said. "Probably bought and paid for."

Clarence's face had turned slightly reddish in color. I had a feeling pissing him off wouldn't be a good idea.

"What is the alibi? Do you know?"

Clarence shook his head. "The cops wouldn't tell me. Said it was an official matter. Official, my ass."

"If you don't know what the alibi is, how can you be so convinced it isn't valid?" I asked.

"Because of what Jesse said," he said. His voice was full of exasperation. I felt like the dumb kid in class and no matter how hard the teacher tried, I just couldn't grasp the concept at hand.

"That he was possessive," Clarence said. "Jealous. Christ, the guy's practically a hermit. Just him, his ship, and dragging dead wood out of the lake. No wonder he latched on to Jesse."

A silence hung in the air for a few moments.

"Are you going to help me?" he asked.

"Here's what I think," I said, leaning forward. "My advice is if you are determined to have the outcome of this investigation be the uncovering of a complex murder plot involving your daughter, don't hire me."

He looked at me, almost a glint in his eye. It reminded me of Clint Eastwood in *Unforgiven*.

"I'm ninety-nine percent sure that if I do further investigation," I continued, "I'm going to find that it was, in fact, a burglary gone wrong. Maybe you'll get mad and won't want to pay me or maybe you'll just try to beat the shit out of me. Whatever. If, however, you truly are interested in uncovering the truth—even if that truth isn't something you agree with—then we can talk. So you tell me what you want out of this, and we'll see what we can work out."

He eased himself out of his chair and walked toward the pictures on the wall. He passed by the ones featuring himself and other celebrities. He paused at the end of the row. I couldn't see what he was looking at. But his big shoulders slumped slightly. For just a moment, he looked like a tired old man.

"My wife was a pessimist," he said. His voice was low and gentle. "Back then, I was just a studio musician and a songwriter doing small solo gigs at backwoods clubs. She was a secretary who came to see me play once. Introduced herself. She was so goddamn beautiful. Blond hair, gray eyes that could twist your insides if she looked at you a certain way. This was before my would-be manager approached me and told me he could make a star out of me. That I was a hit-making machine waiting to be put into production."

I leaned forward in my chair, trying to get a better look at the photos on the wall as he told his story.

"Anyway, we started seeing each other and got married only a few months later," he said. "I was writing, singing, and playing whenever I could. Hell, all the time. But it was just me and her back then. That wasn't just love. It was intense love."

He turned back to me, and his eyes blazed. *Jesus,* I thought, *this guy is old school.*

"See, she didn't want to have kids," he said. "It was that pessimist in her. She thought most people were bastards through and through. A truly low opinion of human nature, of society in general. She was sort of a split personality, which I found very attractive. She had a heart of gold, but her take on the world was that it was the equivalent of a pack of hyenas trying to rip off a chunk of the carcass."

"Why did she think that?" I said.

He just shrugged his big shoulders. "She never really said. I think her parents splitting up had something to do with it. I don't think her childhood was the greatest. But

43

it's not like she was a sad sack either. She was happy go lucky most of the time. But it was hard to get her to give people the benefit of the doubt, you know?"

"I do."

"She loved me, though. I guess she thought I was the exception to the rule."

I nodded. Like so many theories on human behavior, there was a grain of truth to it.

"But when it came to people and the world around me, I was Mr. Fucking Optimistic. The world was my oyster, boy. I knew I could make good music. The future was full of joy, happiness, and success. And money too. To me, that was all a given. But what I really wanted was a family. I wanted kids, man. To me, that was the end all in life. And hell, I didn't think people were all bad. Sure, there were jackals. But there are good people too."

He walked back and sat down in his chair. There were tears in his eyes, and he didn't try to hide them. By now, they were probably old friends to him. "So we had Jesse. And my wife died of cancer a few years later. And now . . . Jesse's gone. I feel like my wife was right. I never should have brought a child into this world unless I could protect that child completely and indefinitely. It's my fault she's dead. I couldn't protect her. But I can find out who did it. Find out which jackal it was. And I can make them pay. It won't bring her back. But . . . I guess . . ." He raised his hands in a gesture of helplessness. "I guess it's all I can do," he said.

I didn't know what to say. I knew what he was going through. I had lost a child too. Not one of my own. But a child I had been responsible for. But I didn't think that would help him. So I kept my mouth shut. Soon he was able to continue.

"So do what you can," he said. "If I'm wrong, I'm wrong. But I want you to leave no stone unturned. Bring me irrefutable proof that it was random and we'll be done. But keep an open mind."

Clarence looked tired and spent. I didn't just want to take the case. I wanted to hug him.

"Okay, deal," I said. "I'd like to get started immediately."

"Just tell me what you need."

"For starters, I want to see her studio."

Nine

In my brief time as a cop, I'd only been to a few crime scenes. To say it's odd is an understatement. It's the little things like inspirational notes tacked on the fridge. Message slips next to the phone. Clothes draped over the back of a chair. Notes and letters and bills and grocery lists. Those are the things that suddenly seem like haunted memories.

Jesse Barre's guitar studio was no exception.

The building was at the end of Kercheval, a stone's throw from the Detroit border. Like just about every other building on this end of town, it had most likely been through many, many incarnations. Restaurants, furniture stores, craft shops, liquor stores. One and all had been tried. The problem was not too many people in Grosse Pointe like coming down for a reminder of just how close they are to the Big D. Especially at night.

Jesse's studio was two stories of sienna-colored brick with a small stone inset at the top reading "1924."

Clarence and I parked then went around to the back. An alley ran behind the building.

"You sure this is okay?" Clarence asked me as we circumvented the police tape stretched across the back door. There was a big square of plywood where a window used to be. Clarence looked at it but didn't say anything.

"Yeah," I lied. "I'm pretty tight with the chief of police."

He nodded. I could see his face, and it didn't look good. Pale, and his jaw was clenched shut.

"Clarence, why don't you wait in the car?" I said.

He shook his head. "I've been in here once already . . . after. I can do this." He unlocked the door, and we stepped inside. I pulled it shut behind us and locked it.

The first thing I noticed was the smell. It smelled like a lumberyard. That wonderful scent of freshly cut wood. The second thing I noticed was that the studio was bigger than it looked from the outside. Along one wall was a row of woodworking machines that to my weekend-carpenter's eyes looked like something only Norm Abraham could understand. I recognized a lathe and a huge old scoping saw, as well as a drill press and table saw, but the rest of them, I had no idea what they did.

Along the other wall was a long workbench, at least twenty feet, with lots of stains and gouges and scratches. It had seen a lot of use in its life. A pegboard hung above it. On the pegboard was a collection of hand tools that looked like they belonged in either an antique store or some kind of torture chamber. I saw more weird-looking clamps and medieval-looking instruments than I knew existed.

At the end of the studio, opposite the entrance was what appeared to be Jesse's main work center. There was a vast array of lights, and a more sophisticated table with an impressive collection of measuring equipment. There was also the only real chair in the place.

Next to the table was the chalk outline of Jesse's final resting place. I imagined her body on the floor, surrounded by the tools of her craft. The fragments of guitar pieces looking down at her. Even though I'm not terribly religious, something like a short prayer vocalized itself in my mind.

Clarence came and stood next to me. I could hear his breathing, labored and rapid. He looked down at the other end of the studio and, after a moment, said with a voice that had lost all of its timbre and conviction, "Maybe I will wait in the car."

I said, "Okay," and waited for him to leave. Once the door was shut, I walked ahead and tried not to dwell on the giant blood stain still visible on the concrete floor.

I made my way around the workshop. I studied the blood spot on the floor then looked at the ceiling. There were blood splatters that had been noted by the crime scene technician. Despite the fact that there was probably no way Clarence could have missed them, I hoped to God that he hadn't seen them. The brutality of the crime shook me. A blood splatter on the ceiling meant that after this woman had had her head cracked open and the blunt instrument was covered in blood, the perp had kept beating. Nothing drives home the violence of a crime like blood splatters on the ceiling.

There were a lot of fragmentary pieces—shapes and contours of wood that would eventually be used in a guitar. I recognized a kind of rib framing and several guitar necks. There were boxes of the knobs guitarists use to tune the strings. Off in one corner were a small sink and an old, battered coffeemaker with a hodgepodge of cups surrounding it. A small refrigerator was tucked beneath a makeshift countertop. On a shelf above the coffeemaker was a dusty stereo with stacks of CDs and audio cassettes. Mostly classical music. The majority of them played on guitar.

It was all mundane and not glamorous in the least bit. But most importantly of all to my way of thinking, it was pretty much useless to a petty thief.

I just stood for a moment in the studio. Outside, I could hear the occasional hum of traffic, maybe a voice here or there. The pipes in the building occasionally creaked and popped. Ordinarily you would probably never hear them. But now in the stillness of the aftermath, they seemed like loud intrusions.

I tried to glean any other pieces of information from the room that I could. I re-examined the point of entry for the killer. Took particular time studying the door and the actual spot of the crime.

I took one final look around the workshop then, satisfied, contemplated what to do next.

Clarence had mentioned to me that Jesse lived above the studio in a simple apartment. As he put it, it hadn't been much, but she hadn't wanted much. I thought of going up to her living quarters but hesitated. Although entering the workshop was technically illegal, it seemed that sneaking into Jesse's living quarters was an even bigger violation, although more of a moral infraction.

The guitar pieces hanging from various hooks and clamps eyeballed me as I wrestled with indecision. In the end, I knew I had to do it. If Clarence really wanted me to find out whether or not his daughter was truly the victim of a premeditated crime, it had to be done.

After all, I'd promised Clarence I would find out the truth.

•

True to Clarence's word, the apartment wasn't much. A living room with simple furnishings: a comfortable but well-worn leather couch, an old Adirondack-style rocking chair, a wall of bookshelves filled with tomes on art and music.

There was an old guitar resting in a stand next to the rocker. It definitely wasn't one Jesse had made. It reminded me of those old jazz numbers from the 1920s. At the top, the name "Gibson" was emblazoned across the wood.

I walked through the living room and into the kitchen. It too was simple with a small pine table and two old, wooden chairs. A stove from the '50s was next to a fridge, most likely from the same decade. To the left of the sink was a small amount of counter and a few simple cabinets painted robin's egg blue. The small butcher block countertop smelled vaguely of red wine and garlic.

A short hallway ran off the kitchen to two bedrooms. One had a small bed with a pine night table. There was a painting over the headboard that looked original. It portrayed a Northwoods Harbor empty save for a few small boats. It looked cold and gray.

The second bedroom was nearly empty save for a few guitar cases, a steel folding chair and a small stereo. There was a bathroom between the bedrooms. I peeked inside and saw that it was small and cramped but impeccably clean.

I walked back to the living room and tried to imagine Jesse Barre, a talented guitar maker, daughter of a talented musician, working all day in the shop, then coming up here to relax. When? Did she eat in the studio or up here? What time did she finish? Dinnertime, or later? Was she a night owl? The living room looked hardly lived in. There was no television. No stereo. Just the couch, the rocking chair, a lamp, and the books. Did she spend all day laboring over the machines, the grinding and cutting and sanding and shaping of wood, then retire up here with a glass of wine and a good book?

Not a bad way to go, really. Awfully solitary though. Was she antisocial? Working all day alone, then coming up here alone? How often did this Nevada Hornsby come by?

I looked around the living room for pictures, spotted a small shelf to the left of the rocker. I crossed the room and studied them. There were about seven all together. All very small frames. There was one of Jesse, who at the time looked to be in her early twenties, with a woman who was considerably older. Her mother. Where was Clarence? I studied the pictures and saw two with him, one younger and one probably a couple years ago.

I heard a footstep behind me.

I picked up the picture and started to say to Clarence, who had probably gotten tired of waiting in the car, "So tell me about this picture—"

The blow came out of the darkness, sent pain shooting through my middle. My kidneys flattened, and I instantly sank to my knees. I tried to turn my head, but a walloping smash that felt like a brick being broken over my head toppled me over onto the floor. Instantly, my attacker was on top of me. He had on a mask. A knife flashed in front of my face, and then I felt its razor sharpness against my throat. I could feel his breath on my face. It smelled like beer and hamburger.

"Where is it?" he asked.

I tried to answer but my tongue and brain weren't connecting. Some kind of wiring had been rearranged.

"Don't play dumb, motherfucker. I'll split you in two right here."

I saw the flash of teeth through the fabric of the mask. I tried again to speak, but nothing came out. I felt blood in my mouth, and there was an enormous pressure against my eyes. My head was going to explode, I was sure of it. Suddenly, he grabbed the neck of my shirt and dragged me across the floor.

"You're going to tell me where it is or you're going to fucking die. Those are your choices."

His voice was raw and angry. He was slightly out of breath. I tried to fight him, tried to raise my arms, but my vision came in bursts, followed by oceans of black. My limbs were numb and useless. I felt myself falling, banging off the stairs, the wall, the handrail leading down into the shop. I saw snapshots of wood and plaster, felt stabs of pain in my back, shoulders, and face. Everything went black. But it was only for a second, because a blurred canvas of colors washed across my brain before I heard his steps and then felt his hands on me again.

There was a roar in my ears, and he pulled me into a sitting position, pinning me against a base cabinet. Now, the roaring was closer and louder. One of my eyes must have already been swollen shut because I couldn't see anything to my left. All I could see out of the other one was the rounded edge of a woodworking machine. He grabbed my right arm and pulled it toward him. He changed his grip, holding two of my fingers in each hand. He pulled them apart so they formed a V, opening up a path that would go directly into the middle of my hand. My fingers were pulled so far apart I was sure he was going to rip them right out of my hand. I twisted as best I could, heaved against him in a panicked fury, but to no avail. He leaned against me, pinning me still, my hand a helpless sacrifice to whatever he intended to do.

"Where . . . is . . . it?" he asked me again. I could practically hear his teeth grinding as the words choked from his mouth.

I turned my head so my good eye could get a better look, and what I saw sent my body and mind both screaming in panic. The roaring was the high-pitched whine of a glorified scroll saw—a thin blade moving up and down with nearly incomprehensible speed. My hand was pressed onto the cutting surface, the blade already in the middle of the V, just an inch or so away from the webbing of where the fingers met the palm.

Before I could react, he pushed my arm forward and a searing pain shot up my palm to my arm to my brain, and I exploded as I saw the blade sink its teeth into my flesh. I crashed against the man, and we both fell against the saw. I felt the blade rip from my hand, and then the man screamed in pain. We both toppled to the floor. I heard his knife clatter across the concrete just before my head banged against the floor, and then he was on top of me, punching and kicking and the lights were swirling.

I lashed out at him, but my blows caught air or glanced off him harmlessly. I was going to die, a few feet from where Jesse Barre's blood still stained the concrete—then the color of the flashing lights changed from a throbbing, dull yellow to bright white.

The blows suddenly stopped, and he was off me in a rush. I struggled to get up, but my legs didn't want to cooperate.

I heard shouting and then glass breaking as the windows and walls of the studio were now awash with incredibly bright light. Maybe this was Heaven. I looked for Jesus, thinking he would wave me in. Instead, I saw a thick wave of gray hair.

"Grandma?" I asked. "Should I come toward the light?"

For just a second, everything started to spin, and the spacious room looked like a dance floor. Only instead of teenagers consumed with the throes of adolescent love, the only thing happening at center stage was a thirty-five-year-old father of two bleeding and overcome with more pain than he'd ever thought possible.

The figure in the light moved and said something I couldn't understand.

Just before I blacked out for good, I figured out who was calling me to Heaven.

It was Kenny Rogers.

Ten

The last time I had stitches, I was eight years old. I'd gone ice skating for the first and last time. I took a header and fell flat on my face, my front tooth slicing through my lip. A lip the size of a ping pong ball resulted, with four stitches sealing up the cut.

Now, at Bon Secour Hospital's emergency room, I got the same number in the middle of my hand.

"That's a really ugly cut," the doctor said to me. "How did it happen?"

"I was building a bird feeder, and I got careless," I said. "I was thinking ahead to the cardinals and blue jays, not about what I was doing."

He nodded like he heard it all the time.

"You know that older guy you came in with?" the doctor asked. "Where do I know him from?"

I sang, "You got to know when to hold 'em, know when to fold 'em, know when to walk away, know when to run . . ."

The doctor gave a surprised look and then peeked out of the room toward the lobby.

"Hey," I said, "Are we done here?"

•

Clarence and I walked out to my car in the Bon Secour Hospital parking lot. My hand had a small bandage, but unfortunately not so small that I'd be able to get it past my wife without her noticing. That would be another tussle where I'd end up on the losing end.

I insisted on driving—no way was I going to let a minor woodworking accident turn me into an invalid. After we got in and I pulled out onto Jefferson, I thought for a moment before speaking. With my hand bleeding so badly, Clarence and I hadn't really had a chance to talk about what happened. Now that I was okay, I needed to hear his side of it.

"So tell me what you saw," I said.

"At first, nothing," he said. "I was fiddling with the radio a lot, trying to find some decent music, but all I kept getting was this synthesized Britney Spears kind of shit. Then I realized I wasn't listening to the radio but one of your CDs."

I could feel his eyes on me, and I visibly squirmed. "I was just making sure it was acceptable for my daughters." God, I hated being busted.

Clarence ignored me and said, "So I finally found a decent country station and laid back and closed my eyes, thought about Jesse."

"Which explains why you didn't see or hear anything."

"And then, I don't know why, but I sat up and looked over, and I thought I saw some shadows moving inside. I mean, it was hard to tell. But even so, it seemed like there were two shadows."

"So you came to investigate."

"I turned off the radio and heard a saw. And I thought, *what the fuck is he doing? Building a coffee table in the dark?* And it kind of pissed me off, that you would feel like you could just turn on one of Jesse's saws. Those things are personal to a craftsman."

"So you . . ."

"So I walked in, thinking you had bumped up against one of the machines and probably couldn't figure out how to turn it off."

"Thanks for the vote of confidence."

"Hey, no offense, but you don't seem like the handy type."

I let that one go and said, "So you turned on the light."

"And the guy was already through the window because I guess he heard me come in through the door. I didn't see anything but blue jeans, a leather jacket, and a ski mask."

I nodded and waited.

"I would have called the cops right away, but I figured we weren't supposed to be there in the first place. I didn't want to get either one of us in trouble."

He had a funny look on his face, and I knew what was coming next before he even said it.

"It was Hornsby. I know it was him."

"But you didn't get a good look," I said.

"It was him. I've met him. Same build. Same movement."

"Was he wearing a ski mask the last time you saw him?"

Clarence didn't say anything to that, but I knew he would claim it was Hornsby. My attacker could have been a black Parisian midget and Clarence would have somehow argued it was Hornsby.

We rode in silence as I drove toward Clarence's house. I wanted to believe him, but Jesus Christ . . . I practically get my hand turned into a dovetail joint and Clarence had no idea anything was going on? Pretty convenient that he had his eyes closed and the radio on. See no evil, hear no evil. I imagined a scenario in which Clarence made a call to someone to come and rough me up. But that was paranoia. Why would he do that? Why would he hire me and then have someone turn me into the classic shop teacher with a missing digit or two?

"What now?" Clarence said.

I pulled into his driveway to let him out.

"Well," I said, "a crime was committed, and I guess I have to report it to the police."

"And then what?"

"Then I talk to Nevada Hornsby."

•

There are three main roads from Detroit that cross the Alter Road border into Grosse Pointe. They are Jefferson, Kercheval, and Mack. There used to be a rumor that at those three main intersections, a Grosse Pointe cop car could always be found, idling, waiting for any Detroiter, most likely with dark skin, to come across the line. At which point, the Grosse Pointe cops would spring into action.

If it ever was true, it certainly wasn't any longer. However, the Grosse Pointe police station, for the part of Grosse Pointe known as the Park, is located just off of Alter Road on Jefferson, one of the main intersections between the two disparate communities. Certainly, a Detroiter would think twice about ambling across the city line on a path that would take him or her directly in front of the cop shop.

I'm sure the location of police headquarters is just a coincidence. Honestly.

Like just about everything else in Grosse Pointe, police headquarters were very clean. The building itself was made of brick that fit nicely into the surrounding architectural style. Inside, the carpet was immaculate, modern desks free of clutter, and a squad room that smelled more like a bank than a home to cops.

Every time I came back, which was quite often, I couldn't help but think of my first day on the force so many years ago. The offices had changed a little, new carpet and paint, different desks, the layout of offices and cubicles had all been changed. But it was the same place. It wasn't as terrifying to me now as it had been back then, when I was a rookie, fresh from the Michigan Police Academy on his first assignment. Back then, I was sweating beneath the dark-blue uniform, my palms slick with nervousness as I shook hands with my new coworkers. My brothers in blue.

It's funny, in retrospect . . . how, when you're nervous, you tell yourself that you're making too big a deal out of whatever's causing your anxiety. You imagine a worst-case scenario and then imagine that it will never get that bad.

It's funny and it's not. Because looking back, I had no idea just how right my fears would turn out to be. And in fact, I hadn't been exaggerating. The truth was, at the time, I was grossly underestimating just how fucked up everything would become. I had low-balled it in a way I never could have conceived.

Now, I walked to the front desk and saw Suzy Wilkins, the receptionist. She was in her mid-forties, a clear, strong face with hair that was shot through with gray. But the steel in her eyes had a way of discouraging any bullshit. Always a good trait in a police department receptionist.

"The Chief in?" I asked.

She nodded, the telephone headset emitting the sound of someone on the other end of the line. She fingered the buzzer beneath the top of her desk, and a deep buzzing sounded as the main door into the squad room unlatched. I walked through the metal reinforced doorway and down the hall. There were framed pictures of the department's officers on the walls, most with commendations for public service, a few for awards. The Chief was pictured in many of the stories and articles, a look of proud stoicism that I knew very well. The Chief hadn't been the chief when I started on the force. That happened a few years after the murder of a certain young man.

I passed a couple of patrol cops in the hallway. We nodded our hellos. It was always a tad awkward. I used to be one of them, but not anymore. They all knew me, knew my story—the most important element being the fact that I had left the force in disgrace. Something they were embarrassed about, and really didn't want to be associated with. Hey, who could blame them? Certainly not me.

I got to the end of the hallway, in the southwest corner of the building, to the Chief's office. I peeked in, saw Grosse Pointe's top cop talking on the phone. The office was big and well ordered. A large oak desk sat along the far wall. A bookshelf ran below the windows facing Jefferson Avenue. Two visitor's chairs faced the desk. On the wall behind the desk were pictures of the Chief winning awards, honors, even a few marksmanship awards. There was also a picture of the family on a low shelf. Nice family. The happy husband and wife, two sons and, the youngest, a daughter. They were three, five, and seven. All spaced sequentially, all products of planned passion. The Chief never did anything half-assed or unorganized. And that applied to procreating.

I sat in one of the chairs and watched the Chief talk on the phone. The voice was always cool and authoritative. Clipped words with precise questions. I had no idea if the conversation was with a convicted felon turned informant, or one of the kids. You could never tell.

Our eyes met, but as usual, the Chief was wearing a game face. No emotions conveyed, not even a recognition of my presence. It's how it worked in the big office. No quarter offered, none given.

Finally the Chief put down the phone and looked at me.

"What's up?" she asked.

"Does something have to be up for me to drop by?"

"Yes. Now what is it? I'm busy."

"You can't talk to me like that."

She rolled her eyes.

Frankly, I didn't care that she was chief of police. She was still my big sister.

Eleven

"Jesse Barre," I said.

"What happened to your hand?" my sister said. Her name was Ellen and she didn't really care about my hand. As police chief, she probably felt like she had to ask. Trust me on this one.

Ellen gave me a bored look that said she knew I was bullshitting her but didn't care enough to pursue it. She was smaller than me but still tall at five foot ten. Dark hair, blue-green eyes. A nice smile she trotted out once a year, maybe.

"Jesse Barre," I repeated.

"What about her?" My sister looked at me, and I knew the expression well. Had seen it in the mirror many times. After all, we looked a lot alike. The only difference was that she was a few years older. A little bit tougher. And a whole lot meaner.

"Was it just a smash-and-grab gone wrong?"

She held out her hands. "Does the phrase 'under investigation' mean anything to you?" My sister wore her I-don't-give-a-shit look that I'd seen many times.

"Yes it does," I said. "It means you didn't answer the question."

Ellen had been made chief of police nearly five years ago. The youngest chief in Grosse Pointe's history. It seemed to surprise everyone but her. And me. She'd managed it well, even with the embarrassment her little brother had brought to the department. In fact, sometimes I believed that my catastrophe, such as it was, had prodded her to work harder and do better. In the end though, it didn't matter. The truth was Ellen was a great cop. Unquestionably the best cop Grosse Pointe had ever had. She alone had earned the top job. And no one questioned that.

"Who's asking?"

I took her question as a good sign. If it was a hot case and progress was being made, she probably would have already shown me the door. My sister doesn't fuck around. So I took the fact that I was still sitting across from her as permission to plow ahead.

"Her father. He wants me to look into it. Figures there's more to it than a burglary gone wrong."

"And his evidence?"

"He loved his daughter. Thinks she was talented. Thinks there's more to the story. Said something about her boyfriend."

Ellen nodded. "Nevada Hornsby. Runs a lumber salvage business in St. Clair Shores. Has an airtight alibi."

"Which is?"

"Which is none of your fucking business."

"Come on, Ellen. It's not like you're letting out the secret to making a dirty bomb. Tell me what his fricking alibi is."

Her phone rang, and she punched it, not gently, sending the caller either into voicemail or, more likely, oblivion.

"He was visiting his sick mother in a nursing home," she said. "Half a dozen witnesses."

I nodded. Night-duty nurses. Other patients. Sounded like a good alibi.

"Don't let the door hit your ass on the way out," my sister said to me.

"Ellen, I'm not here to figure out who killed her. I just want to know if there's going to be a problem with me taking the case."

"What's the deal with your hand?"

"I told you, a paring accident. A kiwi got away from me."

She stood and walked around to the front of the desk. The leather from her gun belt squeaked. She leaned up against the front edge of the rough-hewn wood desk.

"Are you planning on doing anything illegal?"

"No."

"Are you going to call me with anything you find before you call the father?"

"Yes."

She looked me over.

"Kiwi, huh?"

I nodded.

"So it jumped right off the cutting board and slapped you around?"

I pretended to be confused.

"I can see the marks on your face from here, you idiot," she said, "and I can tell by the way you're sitting you've got a couple of sore ribs."

Why do I ever try to lie to her in the first place? So I told her what had happened.

"Jesus Christ, John. You come in to ask me if it's okay to take the case and you already did."

"I still asked."

She rolled her eyes and said, "The old man gave you the keys, so no breaking-and-entering. Tampering with a crime scene, however—"

"There wasn't any tape on the apartment."

"And didn't you learn any self-defense moves at the academy?"

"It wasn't a fair fight, Ellen. He got me from behind, and from then on, I was just a fucking punching bag. Until he tried to saw my hand in half . . . that was enough to clear the cobwebs out."

"So other than an obvious interest in carpentry techniques, what do you know about this guy?" She looked out the small window with a view of Jefferson when she asked—an interrogation technique perhaps? Or was she honestly bored with me?

I shook my head. "Nothing. He had on a mask. He smashed me on the head right away, and after that, everything was kind of dark."

"Rough size?"

"Probably around six feet or an inch or two over it. Solid, but not a huge guy."

She nodded, not bothering to write any of it down. This was all off the record.

"It changes things, doesn't it?"

"Don't fucking flatter yourself."

Her phone rang, and she looked at me. Meeting over.

"So I'm going to keep working on it, okay?"

She went back to her desk and reached for the phone. Ordinarily a sister might suggest that her brother be careful or offer words of encouragement.

Ellen shrugged her shoulders.

"Do what you gotta do," she said.

Twelve

The Rockne residence is a brick colonial on Balfour Road in the Park. When we bought it four years ago, it was a fixer-upper in the classic sense. Bad carpet, a grungy kitchen, horrid paint colors, and pink tile. It took a few years for us to fix it up, but we got it done. Of course, the marriage almost went with it, but we got it done.

My wife's name is Anna. Imagine the stereotypical Italian beauty, and you've got my wife. Big dark eyes, black hair, full features, and a temper that could roast meat. She's tough, sensitive, argumentative, emotional, loving, giving, quick to anger, slow to forgive, frugal with compliments, and sometimes she's just downright nasty. Naturally I love her like the fool I am and wouldn't have her any other way. I tell her I love her more times than she tells me. That's how we are. But she's tougher than I am, so there you go. We have two girls, Isabel and Nina. Isabel's five, Nina's three. They both look just like their Mom, thank God, and naturally I worship them like the miracles they are.

I parked the Taurus in the garage and went inside. Instantly, I wished I hadn't. I could never have an affair because my wife knows exactly what's going on with me in an instant. Because as best as I'd tried to keep my hand hidden from her, Anna spun me around and held my bandage up to the light.

She was definitely not happy. And when she's not happy, no one else in the family is either. It's a scientific impossibility.

"The doctor said it was one of the worst paper cuts he's ever seen," I said.

"A paper cut?" Anna said, repeating my lame improv. The girls were in bed. I was starting to laugh at my wife's expression, but she was clearly failing to find any humor in the situation.

"Yeah, it was that heavy construction paper. You know . . ."

"John . . ."

". . . the kind you used in school with all the colors? It's so thick! It's practically a Bowie knife. You could cut a T-bone—"

Anna glared at me and I stopped talking. There was no getting around it. I was going to have to tell the truth.

"Okay, I was in a bit of a . . . tussle."

"A tussle?"

"Yeah, it's kind of a cross between a tumble and a wrestle. A tussle. From the Latin word tussilius. Meaning to—"

"Shut up."

"Okay."

She tapped her feet and drummed her fingers. She was very coordinated.

"A tussle with who?" she said.

"Some guy."

"Some guy as in some guy you don't know? Or some guy as in some guy you didn't get a good look at?"

"I would say the latter."

"And how did your hand get hurt?"

"Well, we were—"

"Tussling."

"Right. And a woodworking machine got turned on, and we crashed into it, and it went right between my fingers. A freak shop accident. Happens all the time. You ever have a shop teacher? Ever notice how they all have part of a finger missing? In high school my shop teacher was the baseball coach, and one time we asked when practice was, and he held up three fingers but one of the fingers was half gone, so somebody yelled out 'two forty-five?'"

I chuckled, but as Anna wasn't laughing, I quickly stopped.

By now, we were in the living room. Anna sat on the couch, propped her feet up on the ottoman, grabbed a throw pillow, and hugged it to her chest. I gave her a brief overview of the case.

"Did you talk to your sister?"

"Uh-huh."

"And?"

"She said I should do what I gotta do."

This brought an eye roll.

"Look, it was a freak accident," I said. " I'm sure it had very little to do with the case."

"You expect me to believe that?"

"I don't know what to believe right now. I have to keep at it and try to figure out what's going on."

I recognized the look on Anna's face. It was the expression she wears when she wants to tell me to drop this whole PI thing, that I got out of law enforcement for a reason. That what the world really needs is another fucking accountant. She opened her mouth, and I knew she was going to launch into the speech I'd heard quite a few times.

Instead she just shrugged her shoulders, indifferent.

Holy Christ, that was even worse.

•

The next morning I was back in my office, a fresh pot of Peet's coffee (I was on the mailing program—a fresh bag every month straight from Portland, Oregon) and the telephone. I looked up the number for St. Clair Salvage and dialed the number.

There was no answer. I left a message, letting him know that I was a private investigator working for Clarence Barre and that I would like to talk to him about Jesse.

By lunchtime I had finished all of the filing and paperwork I could find around the office and Hornsby still hadn't called me. I left another message, this time alerting Nevada Hornsby to the fact that he had just won a year's supply of a new product called Turkey Jerky—all the great taste of jerky with half the fat and calories. Now available in three flavors: ranch, jalapeño and lemon lime! I left my number and urged him to hurry, hurry, hurry!

By mid-afternoon I had searched the 'net for as much information as I could find on Hornsby. There wasn't much. Just a very short human-interest story in the *Free Press* about St. Clair Salvage. Nothing useful that shed any light on Clarence Barre's enemy number one.

I looked at the clock. It was now dinnertime, and Hornsby still hadn't called me. My next message informed him that a distant relative living in Hawaii had died and left him a forty-eight-acre estate on Maui, complete with three swimming pools, a cabana, and a small population of native island girls who ran the property's private nude beach. All he had to do was call the number (coincidentally, the same one offering a year of Turkey Jerky.)

I used the other phone, my private line, to call Clarence Barre. He answered on the third ring.

"Tell me everything you know about Nevada Hornsby."

I listened while Clarence laid out what he had. It wasn't much. Apparently the guy didn't talk about his past. He was most likely from Michigan. Didn't have family to speak of. Ran St. Clair Salvage and had been in love with his daughter. Like I said, not much.

"I think he's bad. Just a bad, evil person," Clarence said.

There Clarence went again with his intuition. Weren't women supposed to have that? Clarence had more than his share. Maybe he had the stuff I didn't get.

I finished with Clarence and checked the clock. *Quittin' time.*

I went home, had dinner, played with the kids, and then just before going to bed, called in to my answering machine. There still wasn't an answer from the elusive Mr. Hornsby.

I guess I would have to deliver the jerky in person.

Thirteen

The Spook stood before the full-length mirror in his suite at the Royalton Hotel in New York City. His Fender Telecaster was slung over his shoulder, its cable trailing out behind him to the small Pignose amplifier propped up on the bed. He had the guitar's distortion on a medium setting, the juice turned to the first pickup. The settings were designed to create a dense, fuzzy sound that was tight enough to sound like a raucous bouncing romp when he pounded down a blues shuffle.

The Spook put an unlit cigarette in the corner of his mouth and looked at himself in the mirror again. He had just flown in from London via Mexico the night before and looked like an exhausted traveler. He saw a pale man in his late thirties, early forties with scraggly black hair and a thin, pinched, slightly pockmarked face. He had on dirty blue jeans, cowboy boots, a short-sleeved black T-shirt, and a bone necklace.

On his right ring finger was a large skull ring.

The Spook had two loves in the world: the first was the ecstasy of a perfectly executed hit. There was really nothing like it in the world. Scoping things out, identifying the target, waiting for the perfect opportunity. Selecting the absolutely most pristine time and place. And then delivering the knockout blow with strength, speed, and deadly aim.

It was like a beautiful melody to him that ended in a blazing crescendo of blood and violence, capped off by the silent applause of a roaring crowd inside his head.

His second love was Keith Alvin Richards, lead guitarist for the Rolling Stones. The Human Riff, they called him. The man who constantly carried around five or six new songs in his head. If you stopped him in the street, he'd be in the middle of constructing a new song at that very moment.

He was the heart and soul of the Stones.

Granted, Mick had something to do with it. But common wisdom held that Mick was a cold fish.

They said that while Mick *thought* it, Keith *felt* it.

For the Spook, whose own profession required a detached frostiness, he longed to be like Keith, for his job required him to be Mick. Keith's riffs spoke to the Spook. The sexy wail of "Honky Tonk Women," the anthemic call of "Satisfaction." They all kindled a flame in the Spook's soul. He could relate to those riffs. To those sudden bursts of inspiration.

Now, in his hotel room, he slid the fingertips of his left hand slowly up the fretboard of his Fender. The little Pignose amp responded smoothly and quietly. As much as the Spook would have loved to crank it up, it wasn't the time nor the place.

In his apartment in London, he had a soundproof studio in which he would sit for hours and play Keith's riffs, *his* riffs, over and over again, until he had a welt on his chest from the Fender digging in.

The thought of his London flat brought back wonderful memories for the Spook. When he had first gone to London almost fifteen years ago, after quietly leaving the CIA and going freelance, he'd immediately set out for Keith's childhood neighborhood. He was supposed to have been scouting out his target, some ambassador from Libya who his client had deemed it was necessary to terminate.

Instead, the Spook had gone sightseeing. He had gone down to Corningwall Road. Found the ramshackle little house where Keith had spent his first ten years.

The Spook had soaked it up. Had imagined young Keith running around, his wicked smile and nasty vibrations welling up inside him. It had been a truly glorious, happy time for the Spook. On his own, free of the rules and regulations the CIA had imposed upon him. A free agent. Gun for hire.

Now, back in his hotel room, The Spook bowed his head and slipped into the rhythmic chords of "Beast of Burden."

As he played, his boots tapped the thick carpet of his hotel room. He lost himself in the beauty of the evocation. In his mind, he was on stage at Wembley. Mick was in front, strutting across the stage. Ronnie was to his right, smiling, strolling. Wyman was in the back, trying not to be noticed. And Charlie was playing with intensity, his face a mask of indifference.

The Spook's fingers slid carelessly along the strings. His right hand tamped the strings, creating a playful syncopation.

What a thing, the Spook thought. *To be born to do something.* That was the ticket. Keith had been born to write and play music. God had opened his brain and poured in all the ability he could handle.

The Spook had a born talent. Killing people was his reason for existence. Each and every one had been a virtuoso performance. He knew this instinctively. It wasn't arrogance or boastfulness. He was the best there was. He knew it. And those who were in the know knew it too.

In the middle of the song's bridge, the phone rang, but the Spook kept playing. If it was important, they'd call back.

Besides, he had an inkling what the phone call was about.

Or, more accurately, who it was all about.

He smiled at the thought.

I'm just waitin' on a friend.

The Spook closed his eyes and felt the music in him while his mind raced ahead to the thought of who he would most likely kill next.

His old friend.

John Rockne.

Fourteen

My plan was to be like a desperate prostitute: loud, aggressive, and unwilling to take no for an answer. How's that for a positive self-image?

Nevada Hornsby clearly wasn't interested in talking to me. After all, what kind of guy would have no interest in nude native island girls and a year's supply of Turkey Jerky?

I pulled up in front of St. Clair Salvage. A quick visual survey showed that Nevada Hornsby's business was made up of three parts: the factory, the office, and probably out back, the boat.

I got out of the Taurus and walked over to what I assumed was the factory or the main shop area. It was a relatively narrow, but long, aluminum shed. I peeked in the windows and saw power equipment inside, as well as stacked logs. There were giant fans on each side of the long room, I imagined for sucking sawdust out of the building and blowing it into the air like one long, constant sneeze.

I walked over to the office area, which looked even less impressive. It was a weather-beaten structure made of old wood—appropriate, at least—with a cedar shake roof, dirty windows, and a beat-up door. You could pay top dollar at Pottery Barn for that distressed wood look. But here, you just wanted to slap a coat of paint on it.

The door rattled under my knock, but when I listened for an answer, all I heard was the howling of the wind off the lake.

The soot on the windows smeared under my rubbing, but soon I'd cleared a space small enough for a small glimpse into the place. It looked pretty much vacant. A couple chairs here and there, some cardboard boxes, and pieces of wood. There was a doorway that led somewhere, but I couldn't see far enough. Maybe the real office was back there.

I walked around to the rear of the building and saw a long pier that branched off into a T. At the end I saw perhaps the ugliest boat of my life. It was a rusty tub, maybe thirty or forty feet long, with an enclosed cabin and a thin stream of black smoke coming out the back.

Two men were on the pier, untying the thick ropes, and preparing to cast off.

I jogged over, jumped onto the dock, and hustled down to the end of the pier. Looking at the water on either side of me, I saw that it was dark brown. Not exactly snorkeling territory here.

I got the attention of one of the men, a reddish-haired guy with a red flannel shirt, jeans, and a wad of chewing tobacco that distended the entire right side of his face.

"Nevada Hornsby?" I asked.

He motioned with his thumb toward the cabin of the boat. It was like a little cubicle that someone had placed in the middle of the boat. It had a little door and little windows that were black with grime.

In the back of the boat was a giant hook-and-pulley system, I assumed to help haul logs out of the lake. There was other equipment scattered around the deck: blocks and pulleys, hooks, big, odd-shaped pieces of steel. Most of it looked entirely unfamiliar to me. Then again, I majored in criminology not mechanical engineering.

The man to whom I'd spoken made no move to get Hornsby for me, but merely went to a different part of the ship and began fiddling with some levers.

I hesitated. The water next to the dock looked cold and unforgiving. I thought briefly of my car, still warm from the heater, a stainless steel coffee mug still half full, nestled in the driver's side cup holder.

Life is full of tough decisions.

I jumped on board.

I made way across the deck and peeked inside the ship's cabin. Nevada Hornsby sat at the small Formica table that jutted out from the side of the cabin's wall.

He was tall and broad-shouldered, with a thick black sweater, blue jeans, and black boots. His thick, dark hair and beard were neat and smooth. The only sign of age and a hard life were the wrinkles around his eyes.

There was a knife in his hand, a long, crude thing that he was using to cut an apple. He looked up at me, the deep blue of his eyes seeming to leap from the weathered face and dark hair.

"Nevada Hornsby?" I asked.

He looked me up and down, and the look in his eye wasn't flattering. He seemed to contemplate the knife in hand for a moment. I got the feeling the knife had gutted a lot of fish and that it could do the job on a private investigator just fine. But his expression didn't come across as anger or violence. It seemed more like . . . weariness.

"My name is John Rockne," I said. "I'm a private investigator. I'd like to ask you a few questions about Jesse Barre."

He got to his feet smoothly, and I quickly saw that he was bigger than I'd imagined. At least six feet four inches. His shoulders seemed bigger too. Fuck, he was just plain big.

I pictured the man who had attacked me at Jesse Barre's apartment. I suddenly had doubts that it could have been Nevada Hornsby. The guy in front of me was too damn big. If he'd wanted to saw my hand in two, he could have done it. Easily.

"Who you workin' for?" he said. He still had the knife in one hand, the apple in the other.

I sort of scrolled through my typical responses, the ones I've spouted maybe a few hundred times in my career. That's confidential. An interested party, etc. They suddenly seemed like they would sound hollow and flimsy in this man's presence. So I went with the truth.

"Clarence Barre."

His face registered nothing, but he did give a slight nod. He worked the knife through the apple and popped a chunk into his mouth.

"I'm leaving in thirty seconds," he finally said. "You can talk to me when I get back."

"How long are you staying out?"

"Eighteen hours."

"Are you sure you don't have a minute to talk?"

He shook his head *no* and stared at me.

"Randy called in sick," he said. "More work for me and Rollie."

"What if I came along?" I said, thinking eighteen hours was a motherfuck of a long time, but if I had to do it, I would.

Hornsby nodded as if he'd known all along that was going to be my response. "If you stay, you work," he said.

I didn't like the sound of that. I had a feeling the lumber-recovery profession was a pretty dangerous job, probably second only to road construction workers in Cairo.

Of course, Hornsby could stay out for a lot longer than eighteen hours—days, even weeks—or just motor up to some other harbor in some other town and I'd never see him again. Or at least not for a long time.

"Ten seconds," he said. He flipped a few switches and looked back at me.

"Aren't we going to talk about my hourly rate?"

"Zero dollars an hour. Anything else?" He revved the engines for emphasis.

"Do you have a 401(k)?" I said.

His response this time was to jam the throttle down. I stumbled backward, knocking his Styrofoam coffee cup off the low shelf next to the table.

"You better have workers' comp!" I yelled over the screaming engines.

I struggled to my feet to say something to him, but he was gone. My eyes were drawn to a picture on the wall that he had been blocking.

It was old and hung in a cheap frame, but there was no mistaking the woman caught on film.

It was Jesse Barre.

Fifteen

"There she is," Hornsby said, his voice a dull growl, not quite as deep as the sound of the ship's engines.

I looked out through the streaked windshield and saw the second ugliest water vessel known to man.

This beast looked like a giant concrete block with an angled front and square back. Its surface was virtually empty save for the roughly fifteen-foot crane standing in the middle. It sat on top of the dark greenish-brown water, rocking gently in the three-foot waves, the sky a solid sheet of gray overhead. Not exactly a Norman Rockwell scene.

Looking back, I couldn't see any signs of land. We were a long way out.

It had been nearly an hour since Hornsby's sudden burst of acceleration had thrown me off my feet. He'd said little more than to tell me we were going out to a barge he used to retrieve sunken lumber. The rest of the ride, he'd ignored my questions.

Now, Hornsby and his worker, Rollie, lashed the boat up against the barge. A few minutes later, Rollie emerged in a wetsuit. I watched him spit out his giant ball of chewing tobacco. It landed in a little metal pail. He set it against the side of the cabin. Ooh, leftovers.

Rollie then went over the side into the water while Hornsby jumped between the two vessels and immediately began hauling a chain and rigging harness to the side of the barge. When Rollie reemerged from the water, Hornsby fed him the chain.

"Is there anything I can do to help?" I said. After all, he'd given me the big lecture about working.

"Yeah, keep out of the way," Hornsby said.

Right. I could do that.

So I watched, waiting for the right moment to begin questioning Hornsby about his relationship with Jesse Barre. I was here to get some goddamn answers. I would be pretty pissed if I spent all day on the S.S. *Piece of Shit* with nothing to show for it but the vague smell of dead carp.

After a few minutes of feeding the chains into the dark water, Hornsby stopped. He stood there, looking down for several minutes. Finally, after Rollie disappeared back into the olive-green depths, I took my opportunity.

"So you know, Clarence thinks you killed her." I figured what the hell, he wasn't answering my questions, maybe I could goad him into talking.

The wind ruffled his dark brown hair, and he smirked. Well, there went that plan. Pissing him off wasn't going to be easy.

A flock of gulls screamed overhead, and Hornsby stepped closer to the edge of the boat.

"He loved his daughter, I'll give you that," he said. "But he never understood her."

"What didn't he understand?"

He waved me away like it was a question not worth answering. After a few minutes of staring into the water, though, he did give me an answer.

"He thinks she wanted to leave me, right?"

I waited, not wanting to divulge anything he didn't already know.

"You don't have to answer. I know I'm right." He walked along the deck of the barge to the base of the tower, with me right on his heels. He put his hands on some of the crane's levers and made a few adjustments.

Overhead, I heard the creak of old machinery beginning to awaken.

"So maybe you're right," I said. "Do you want to deny it?"

"I want to tell you and Clarence to go fuck yourselves, but I can't," he said. "Well, you I can. But not Clarence. She was crazy about him. I wouldn't want to do anything that would upset him. If Jesse were here, that's what she'd be saying."

I took a closer look at him, at his eyes, and for some reason, I believed him. Maybe it was the way he said it. Maybe he was just a helluva good actor. Or maybe it was the dark circles under his eyes, the tired, beaten look in his face. It rang true. It looked like the face of a man who'd just lost the woman he loved.

"So why does he think she was leaving you?" I said.

"Who says she wasn't?"

Okay, he had me there.

"Can we stop playing games?" I asked. "Was she leaving you?"

"She was and she wasn't."

I sighed and looked out toward the lake. The wind shifted a bit, and a giant wave crashed over the side of the barge. I looked down and the front of my Dockers were wet, like I'd pissed my pants. I glanced at Hornsby. He was dry.

"She was and she wasn't?" I said. "What's that supposed to mean?" I walked to Hornsby's left, trying to get a glimpse of what he was doing. I heard a noise overhead and then Hornsby grabbed me. I thought he was going to throw me in the water. But he pushed me forward just as a large pool of heavy chain dropped onto the deck from the crane overhead. It landed right where I'd been standing.

"Shouldn't I be wearing a hard hat?" I said. "I'm a bleeder."

Hornsby appeared not to have heard what I said, nor did he seem to notice the fact that he'd just saved me from grave injury.

"She was taking a sabbatical," he said. "From the shop. From Grosse Pointe. And from me. But she was coming back. She said so. I think she told the old man too." He laughed. "I just don't think he believed her."

"What was she going to do on this . . . sabbatical?"

"I'll tell you when we're done," he said, gesturing toward the water. I looked down, and the first log was ascending to the surface, like an ancient submarine finally coming to port.

"Stay out of the way," he told me. No problem, Ahab.

The chain around the log was hooked to a winch, and Hornsby crossed the deck, released the chain from the winch, and Rollie, in the water, backed away from the log then disappeared.

Hornsby walked back to the crane's control center, fired it up, and slowly maneuvered the big arm out over the water. He spread the clamping mechanism open, brought it down on top of the log, closed it, and hoisted the three-ton, four-hundred-year-old log onto the surface of the barge.

It lay there, still, like a harpooned whale. It was dark brown with a tinge of green on it. Hard to believe beautiful wood could come from that.

This procedure repeated itself over and over again, so that by the time an hour had passed, I felt like I'd learned all I could about the fascinating world of lumber recovery. In other words, I was ready for a nap.

I walked back across the barge, jumped onto the deck of the ship, and went into Hornsby's cabin.

Protected from the wind, it immediately felt warmer, and I helped myself to a cup of coffee from the pot next to the captain's chair. I was so tired the caffeine stood no chance of keeping me awake.

I took the opportunity to look around. There wasn't much for me to snoop through. Some topographic maps of the lake's bottom. Pictures of Hornsby and his crew. A newspaper article on Superior Salvage Company. A few photographs taped to the wall. In one of them, I saw a grinning Hornsby with his arm around Jesse Barre. They both looked comfortable with each other. Relaxed. Maybe even in love.

I found the head, which was surprisingly clean, and took a leak. I went back to the cabin and drained the rest of my coffee. I looked out over the water; a fine mist was thick in the air. It had gotten colder as well. No time to be out on the deck of a barge, that's for sure. You know those guys who loved to be out and fighting the elements? Looking Mother Nature in the eye? I was not one of them. I figured my ancestors worked hard to figure out that it was safer to hide in caves. It would be an insult to their hard work and dedication to be outside right now.

A small cot lay along the opposite wall of the cabin. I stretched out on it, zipped my coat up all the way to my chin. The coffee had momentarily warmed my insides, and I figured that I wouldn't miss much if I took a quick nap.

Besides, I reasoned, I'm a light sleeper.

•

I dreamed of a nice gnocchi dinner, served by my wife whose attire consisted of fishnet stockings and a jaunty beret. She was just about to suggest dessert when something odd happened. Instead of a pleasant garlic aroma, the gnocchi smelled like gasoline.

My eyes opened, and I was suddenly wide awake, scared, and disoriented all at the same time.

I was on Hornsby's boat, in the cabin, and my mind tried to take in the fact that it was nearly dusk and that I must have been sleeping for nearly five hours. Holy Christ, what a fuckup I was.

The early morning had really done me in. I vaulted over the deck of the ship onto the barge. I jogged to the crane control and the area where the chain and harness were, but I saw no one.

I walked to the edge of the ship and looked into the water.

Rollie was on his back, a thick length of the chain tied around his neck. His face was bobbing in and out of the water. His lifeless eyes were bulging, his mouth an open container. Water poured in, water poured back out. A huge log was in the water next to him, and the chain seemed to be holding Rollie alongside.

I looked around the barge, out toward the water. "Hornsby!" I called.

Just as the last echoes of my voice were carried away by the wind, I heard what sounded like a small explosion. More of a whooshing sound. And then the deck of the barge was a column of flame headed right for me. A motor gunned, and I saw a shadow crouched at the throttle of a small outboard, and then I was leaping from the barge, out into Lake St. Clair.

I hit, and the shocking cold of the water made me nearly want to scream.

I went straight down into the water, the sudden silence shocking me as much as the knifing cold.

My jacket weighed a ton, but I kept it on; instead I kicked off my shoes and pants, holding my breath for as long as I could before I had to surface.

When my lungs were burning and I was on the verge of inhaling a mouthful of water, I broke through to the water's surface. Smoke was everywhere. It was like night had come and thrown a stinky blanket over everything. As I struggled to get my bearings, a huge explosion rocked the air. I looked and could just make out through the smoke that Hornsby's boat was now on fire.

I swam toward Rollie. When I was close enough, I put a hand on the log and tried to get a grip on its slick surface. It was difficult, but at last I found a small notch that served as a handhold.

I tried to think things through.

They had killed Rollie and were trying to destroy the ships. So the question was: where was Hornsby?

Despite the situation, I felt a tug of relief. They, whoever that might be, probably weren't after me. If they didn't know I existed, they probably wouldn't come back to try to kill me.

Which was good.

The bad part was, I had no way of getting back to shore, and my body was already going numb from the cold. I had to get out of the water, and get out fast. Then I had to figure out a way to signal someone back on shore.

And there was still no sign of Hornsby.

Part two of the good news was that I knew the barge was virtually indestructible, unlike Hornsby's ship. So when I spied the chain leading from Rollie's neck to the side of the barge, I knew I had a chance. My hands already felt like frozen claws, so I would have to go as quickly as possible. I kicked off from the log, my clothes pulling me under, my body underestimating the strength it would take to keep me afloat and propel me the twenty feet I needed to cross to get to the chain.

I pushed and kicked, the water tugging at me, the cold washing over me. I felt the chain brush my fist. I grabbed for it and missed, immediately going under and getting a mouthful of Lake St. Clair. The parallel with water going in Rollie's mouth inspired me to panic. I flailed back to the surface and got both hands on the chain. I pulled myself to the barge and tried to lift myself from the water, but my jacket and sweater weighed me down. It was going to be impossible. I was going to die, clinging to the chain for a while, like Leonardo de Caprio in *Titanic*, and then I was going to lose my grip and slip to the bottom, landing in a pile of wooden logs.

A giant motherfucker of a wave knocked me against the side of the barge, and I lost any oxygen that was left in my lungs. I gasped for breath, clawed at the chain, and maybe gained a foot or two.

But it was enough.

A red lever hung just below where I needed to get in order to haul myself out of the water.

It was the power switch for the winch.

My body shook with cold, and the exertion of swimming had left my muscles numb with fatigue. I thought of Anna and the kids back home, probably sitting down to dinner, oblivious to the fact that Daddy was hanging on for dear life in the middle of a freezing cold lake, clinging to a boat that was on fire.

The lake seemed to surge beneath me, pushing me toward the winch's control panel. My hands slid up the chain. I grabbed the lever and brought it down, instantly sending the chain into action. The winch pulled it to the surface of the barge, me along with it. I rolled onto the deck and gasped for air. I couldn't believe I'd made it. That I was alive. No life insurance check for Anna. She'd be pissed.

A sudden loud thud made me get to my hands and knees and peer over the side of the barge.

It was the log that Rollie had been attached to. The winch, still winding, had brought it all the way to the side of the ship.

But Rollie was nowhere to be seen.

Something was pinned to the bottom of the log, had been trapped out of sight beneath the water.

Nevada Hornsby.

Sixteen

I'd always wanted to meet someone from the Coast Guard. Somehow, I figured it would be a Saturday field trip with my daughters. I'd call ahead, arrange a tour of the Coast Guard place with some guy called Captain Happy, the girls could pretend to steer the ship, we'd get some fake medals, and then we'd all take pictures and drink cocoa.

Alas, Captain Happy turned out to be a grumpy, middle-aged man, who, after a bumpy ride across Lake St. Clair with two men wearing sidearms giving me the cold stare, unceremoniously deposited me with the St. Clair Shores police. Apparently emergency calls regarding an abundance of dark smoke on Captain Happy's lake didn't inspire a warm, fuzzy feeling in the Coast Guard official. No cocoa, and he never even let me steer the ship. Good thing I hadn't brought the girls along.

The cops escorted me to an ambulance that took me to a hospital, where, after a blatantly cursory inspection, doctors determined I was fine. They didn't even give me the 'twenty-four-hour observation' demand.

The cops then escorted me back to the station where all kinds of phone calls were made, some in my presence, most occurring, I'm guessing, while I waited in a conference room. A couple of St. Clair Shores cops took my statement. Then they re-took it. And then, to qualify for the hat trick, they took it again. I kept it not pretty much the same, but exactly the same.

After they left, I took stock of my situation. The hospital had given me some doctor's scrubs, and my wet clothes were in a paper bag that was now soggy. I had a blanket around my shoulders and was trying to stay warm. I was also trying not to think about Nevada Hornsby, the sight of him lashed to the bottom of the log, his dead eyes staring up at me—

The door banged open and my sister walked in.

She took a moment to look at me. Not a glance. A slow, thorough assessment. When she was done, she turned back toward the door.

"Let's go," she said.

•

I'd found it a pretty good idea when dealing with my sister that if you were not sure what to say, keep it zipped. So I sat in the front passenger seat of her cruiser, looking out the window as we left the hospital parking lot, heading back, I assumed, to my house.

"Listen, I can explain," I said, ignoring my cardinal rule. Why do I even bother to make them up when I so rarely follow them?

"No, you can't," Ellen said.

See what I mean? I cursed myself for ignoring myself.

"I told you what I was doing," I said. Another mistake. Don't defend yourself. Just curl up and let the grizzly bat you around a little bit—eventually she'll get bored and move on.

"You told me you were going to be involved in a double homicide while investigating the homicide I'm working on?" she said. Boy, her voice could sound nasty. It was hard to believe we were related. I guess I got all the sugar, she got all the vinegar. I'd have to get confirmation on that from Mom.

"Do I look like Dionne Warwick?" I said.

She shot me a confused glance.

"Psychic Network?" I said.

This got me an eye roll. Eye rolls aren't bad. In fact, they're quite good. It usually means the anger-bordering-on-violence has passed, replaced with a mere case of irritation. A mild nuisance.

Ellen turned onto Kercheval, headed back toward the Park. It was early evening by now, and traffic was light.

"Where was the call to let me know you were going to question Hornsby?"

"Again," I said, "how was I supposed to know anything would come of it—"

"You're going to back off of this case," she said. I knew where that expression "iron in her voice" came from. She practically had a crowbar between her teeth.

I didn't answer, suddenly terribly interested in the architecture of the houses we passed. After a couple more blocks, Ellen turned onto my street.

"Aren't you, John?" she said.

"Aren't I what?"

"Going to back off this case this minute."

I didn't want to answer. I'd made enough mistakes. I wasn't about to make the granddaddy mistake of all by lying to her. Because I had no intention of backing off this case. In fact, my intention was just the opposite.

"Right?" Ellen asked, not letting me off the hook as we pulled into my driveway.

I imagined a newborn baby, the very picture of innocence. "Right," I said. What the hell, three mistakes in a row. Pulled a hat trick myself.

•

Before I got out of the cruiser, I glanced in the little mirror attached to the back of the sun visor. I looked okay, considering what I'd been through. Pale, water-logged, and truth be told, a tad frightened.

"Does she know?" I said, nodding toward the house. My cell phone was on the bottom of Lake St. Clair, and I hadn't called from the hospital, preferring to tell my wife about my unique day in person.

"I didn't tell her," my sister said.

"Good. Your tact typically leaves quite a bit to be desired."

"Quit stalling," Ellen said. "Go on, take it like the man you aren't."

I got out, slammed the door shut as a response, and walked around the house to the back door. In my mind, I ran through a series of explanations, deciding that I'd already lied to my sister, but lying to my wife would be even worse. No way was I going to lie. I might sanitize the truth a tad, but no more outright lies. Besides, I'd tried a fib or two to Anna before—no, I hadn't eaten the last two chocolate chip cookies, etc.—and I always got busted. The woman was a walking polygraph machine.

I unlocked the back door, which opens into the kitchen, and Anna was at the kitchen table, helping Isabel with her homework. She looked at me then did a double take.

"Everyone's favorite man is home!" I sang out, my voice as merry as an elf on Christmas Eve.

I saw the cold fury in my wife's eyes and I knew it was game over. "Isabel, go upstairs," Anna said. "Finish your math sheet in your room."

After my daughter left—without a hug for her Dad, I might add—Anna folded her arms, waiting.

I began describing what happened, editing out the worst moments. I was only about halfway through the story when Anna started crying, and I immediately started feeing guilty. The girls ran down from upstairs upon hearing the sound of a grownup crying.

"Mommy, what's wrong?" Isabel said, her lower lip immediately starting to tremble.

Anna was trying to get herself under control but failing miserably. I idly wondered when I would get my framed certificate proving once and for all that I was, in fact, the world's biggest jackass.

I decided to divide and conquer. Leaving Anna in the kitchen, I took the girls upstairs, immediately distracting them with a game of tackle and tickle, then we read some books and I tucked them in for the night.

I went back downstairs and found Anna drinking. Turning to booze was always a bad sign. But a small glass of Amaretto wasn't a bad thing. I splashed a cocktail glass half full.

"Finish the story," she said as I sat down on the couch next to her.

I told the rest of it to Anna, glossing over the part where I'd almost been blown to a million pieces of man gnocchi and minimizing how close I'd come to drowning. I told her exactly what the doctors had said, embellishing only on the soundness of my overall health. Still, she was pissed. Whenever she got upset, she cried first then got pissed right after that. Super pissed, in fact.

"Why didn't you take your sister with you?" she said. You have to understand, she was mad, but she wasn't mad at the guy who tried to kill me. She was mad at me.

"She's a cop, honey," I said. "She can't just take off with her brother when he's got a case. Besides, I had no idea this was going to happen. I thought it would be a routine interview. As boring as those Barbara Walters specials. Do you remember the one with Bo Derek? God that was—"

"What about Nate? Why didn't you take him?"

"Nate?" I said. "Well, he's best in culinary emergencies . . . you know, when you can't decide whether to have the roast duck or the broiled flounder."

"This isn't funny."

"I know." It wasn't. The part about Nate was a little bit funny, but no, the rest was definitely not.

"So what are you going to do?" she said.

"I'm going to keep working," I said. She nodded. Anna now knew the details of the case, was caught up in it nearly as much as I was, and she probably didn't want me to stop.

"I just want you to be more careful. Call Ellen if you think you're going to be in any kind of danger, all right?"

"All right."

"Because you know, you're not a tough guy. You're no Russell Crowe."

I took that one in stride. "Very true. Very true."

All in all, I thought it had gone pretty well. Anna didn't seem too unhappy. I was safe. I would be more careful. I would get to the bottom of all this, and it would be a good case to solve.

Things were going to be okay.

Seventeen

Muddy's Saloon is a blues bar just a stone's throw from the Detroit River. All of the greats have played there, leaving behind them the wail of a blues shout and a framed, signed picture.

The Spook stood in the lobby and looked at the pictures. John Lee Hooker, young and handsome with a sharp-looking felt hat and thick, black sunglasses. Elmore James with his lean face and hawk nose. B.B. King and Lucille. Howlin' Wolf. And Muddy himself.

The Spook walked through the doorway to the right of the bar to the small room in back with the stage. It had a small wooden platform with a dozen tables scattered around in front. Thick cigarette smoke filled the air, and the wood floor breathed with the smell of thirty years worth of spilled beer.

The stage itself was only up a step or two, and it had a piano in one corner, a big mahogany upright that probably weighed a ton or two. There were two microphones at the front, and an old wooden stool sat in the middle.

The Spook had been to Detroit before. Quite a few times, in fact. After leaving the Agency and going freelance, some of his first jobs had been right here. There always seemed to be a lot of open contracts in Detroit.

In fact, it was on one of his first jobs that he'd heard about open mic night at Muddy's Saloon. Back then, though, he'd been too busy to attend. Tonight was different. His job hadn't officially started yet, which gave him a rare night off. He'd brought his guitar and was ready to play.

Half of the tables were occupied, mostly by other players, although the Spook noticed one table with a man and a woman sharing a pitcher of Heineken.

A man was on stage playing a serviceable Taj Mahal tune. His accompaniment was simple, his voice good if a bit tentative. The Spook took a seat and ordered a beer. He would hardly touch it.

Two songs later, the man on stage hit the last note of a Howlin' Wolf song and quietly put away his guitar and left the stage. The Master of Ceremonies, a big, pudgy white guy with a fedora and black shirt, asked the audience who would like to play next.

The Spook immediately stood and headed for the stage.

"All right! We got an eager one!" the MC said.

The Spook slid the Martin guitar from its case and tuned by ear. He slid into the "Midnight Rambler" shuffle, and everything felt good. Felt tight.

"Have you heard about the Midnight Rambler?" he sang. His voice wasn't great. He had more of a growl than a true singing voice, but it was his playing that he was most proud of anyway. He played, his rhythm line aggressive and precise.

His intense concentration was broken slightly by something on the periphery of his awareness. He heard the man at the table with the woman snicker softly.

The Spook ignored him, turned back into himself and sang, "The one you never seen before." His foot tapped the oak floor, and the Martin bounced on his thigh. He rocked through the song, feeling strong and confident. When he finished muted applause broke out.

And then the man at the table spoke. Not real loud, but loud enough for most of the people in the room to hear. "Pick a key and stick with it, man!" A little bit of soft laughter broke out.

The Spook ignored him, and did two more numbers: "The Spider and the Fly," and "Love in Vain."

When he stepped down from the stage, the man at the table who'd heckled him earlier clapped especially loud.

The Spook sat back down at his table. He quietly put the Martin back into its case and wrapped his fingers around his beer, but didn't take a drink.

He watched as an obese woman with a jumbo acoustic played a haunting version of a Son House song. Her guitar playing was basic, but her voice was beautiful. The man at the table who'd heckled the Spook was ignoring her, concentrating on the woman at the table with him. The Spook studied the man. He had on a white shirt and tie, slicked back hair, and glasses. He looked like an accountant. Something shifted inside the Spook's stomach. For the first time, he took a sip of beer.

The heckler ordered another pitcher of beer from the waitress and then excused himself from the table. The Spook waited while the man passed by the table and out the door to the bathroom.

After a moment, the Spook picked up his guitar case and followed. He leaned his case against the jukebox just outside the door to the bar and went to the men's room. He stepped inside, shut the door, and stood with his back against it as he slid the Ruger automatic out of his jacket's inside pocket. He lifted the silencer from the other jacket pocket and quickly screwed it onto the end of the pistol. There was only one stall in the bathroom and no urinal. The Spook listened to the man finish up. The stall door swung open, and the accountant appeared. He looked up at the Spook, then away, then back again. An O formed on his mouth as he saw the gun. He started to raise his hands.

The Spook shot him twice in the face.

The man fell back into the stall. The Spook stepped in, placed the barrel of the gun against the man's skull, and fired once more. He then slipped the gun back into his pocket, hoisted the dead man onto the toilet, and shut the stall door.

From the doorway, it looked like just another guy taking a crap.

The Spook walked back to the door, picked up his guitar case, and stepped outside. As the door swung shut, he heard the faint voice of the obese woman singing, "Nobody knows you when you're down and out . . ."

Ain't that the truth, he thought.

Eighteen

I attended a seminar once. It was hosted by a private investigator, and believe me, I know a write-off when I see it. Anyway, the seminar was put on by a woman from Los Angeles who claimed to work for celebrities and had, at least according to herself, been involved with some extremely big, high-profile cases. I suppose when an actress insures her left ass cheek for five million dollars, they probably hire a lot of security personnel.

I ponied up the three hundred bucks for an afternoon of learning the tricks of the trade from one of the self-proclaimed experts in my field. Personally, I thought the woman was worthy of investigation herself, but I could be rather skeptical. And as a con, wouldn't it be a hoot to pull the wool over the eyes of a room full of wannabe private investigators? Reference check, anyone?

Anyway, I remembered laughing out loud at one of her points. She had quizzed the audience about what abilities we felt were the most important for a PI to possess. The crowd threw out self-delusional concepts such as courage, tenacity, and perceptiveness.

It turned out the correct answer was the ability to listen.

I couldn't help it. I started laughing. It just sounded so New Age to me. I mean, I understood her point and all, but I just pictured myself in my office, acting like Bob

Newhart. A client tells me his wife is cheating on him and I say, "Go with that. How does that make you feel? I'm listening, friend."

Listening? Come on. I would have guessed the most important ability was to be able to photograph both faces of two people fucking.

Of course, like so many things in life, over time the concept kind of grew on me. The more cases I had, the more times I realized that something I'd heard ended up playing a pretty big role in the case. So maybe the afternoon had been worth a little more than a sore ass and a few glasses of watered-down Coke.

I thought of the seminar when I realized that something Nevada Hornsby had said to me, that really hadn't registered then, was now simmering on my brain. At the time, I hadn't really been listening. But now, I knew I had. Because he had told me something important.

It was just before he slammed the boat into gear. He'd said something about we'd be out there for eighteen hours and that I would have to work because someone had called in sick. Now I searched my brain for the name. Had he said a name? I thought about it, cursing that hotshot from L.A. I never should have laughed at her. Karma.

Rudy.

No, that didn't sound right. But it had definitely started with an R. I was sure of that.

Ralphie.

Rodney.

Randy.

Randy.

That was it.

Randy had called in sick the day the boat blew up and everyone but a scared PI died. I'd always been wary of coincidences and that was just too glaring for me to take in stride. Maybe I'd host a seminar one day and make that *my* big point.

Fortunately, during my questioning with the good police officers of St. Clair Shores, this particular memory had yet to surface. Somehow, now that I'd had some time to recover from the initial shock, it just popped right up. I'd even been with my sister and still hadn't remembered it then either. Coincidence or had some small part of me repressed the idea until I could act on it alone?

Go figure.

Since I had failed to remember this little detail during my official questioning, it didn't seem like a terribly significant slighting of protocol if I were to look into this Randy angle by myself.

I may not be the best listener in the world, but I am one hell of a rationalizer.

•

My first challenge was to find out just who this Randy guy really was and where I might be able to find him.

I pulled up across the street from St. Clair Salvage. I didn't feel any post-traumatic stress from my near brush with death, but I wasn't exactly doing cartwheels over being back. And having finished going through Jesse Barre's workshop and apartment, I wasn't thrilled at being back at another murder victim's place of work. Again, I wasn't the most sensitive guy in the world, but this case was really starting to get to me.

In the gray light of early morning, with a fog rolling in from the lake, the bright yellow police tape over the front door of St. Clair Salvage made the message pretty clear. Everyone stay away. Especially nosy private investigators.

In the old days, I suppose a ballsy investigator might pick a lock or slip through an old window into Hornsby's office and check his employee records. But I had a couple problems with this. One, I wasn't anxious to break any laws. The guys at Jackson State Prison just a half hour away would love my soft white ass. It'd be like chucking a Krispy Kreme donut into an Overeaters Anonymous meeting.

Second of all, and not quite as anally intrusive, I figured Nevada Hornsby's records were about as neat and organized as a frat house after Rush Week. In fact, I highly doubted that Hornsby kept any employee records at all. No W-2s, no problems from the IRS, right? I pictured him paying cash under the table, along with a few beers and a greasy burger at the café across the street.

The café across the street. It was a Ram's Horn. I'd eaten once at a Ram's Horn. Runny eggs, soggy hash browns, weak coffee. It was one big room with no dividers between the tables. The culinary equivalent of a pig's trough to an uppity Grosse Pointer like myself, but nirvana perhaps to Hornsby and his crew.

I locked the Taurus, crossed the street, and went through the restaurant's fingerprint-covered glass door. A cute, chubby waitress took my order of coffee with a pleasant little smile. She had a dimple and a nametag telling the world her name was Gloria. I sipped my coffee. It was weak, all right. Kind of like coffee-flavored water. When she returned to refill me, I ordered the Hungry Man Special, figuring she might be a little more cooperative if a slightly larger tip were at stake. Fifteen percent of a fifty-cent coffee wasn't about to loosen her up.

When Gloria came back in an astonishingly quick five minutes, burdened down like a pack mule with my Hungry Man Special, I said, "Hey, I was supposed to meet a guy for breakfast. He worked at the salvage shop across the street. His name is Randy. Do you know him?"

Gloria's face blanched a little bit. "Did you hear about the accident?" she said.

"What accident?"

"Their boat blew up. The owner and one other guy died."

"Was it Randy?"

"I don't know."

She unloaded her arm full of platters onto the table. It was like a dump truck raising its bed and a ton of gravel sliding down to the pavement. The smell of grease was intense and, in a morbid kind of way, somewhat alluring. I made my face good and thoughtful. "I wonder how I could find out if Randy's okay."

"Don't you have his phone number or something?"

I shook my head. "I bumped into him at a bar. I overheard him telling someone he worked for some place that salvaged old lumber. I'm remodeling my kitchen, and the better half wants something fancy for the cabinets, so I introduced myself and he said he could hook me up with a good price, but we'd have to make it look like he was buying the cabinets, for the discount, you know? So we agreed to meet here and talk."

Gloria seemed to buy it. The dimple kind of faded in and out while I talked. I wondered if it was a tell, kind of like full dimple for when she believed me, less dimple for skepticism. If so, I was doing pretty well.

"You should talk to Michelle," she said. Full dimple. I was golden. "Those guys came in here once in a while, but they always wanted Michelle to wait on them."

"Okay. Is she working today?"

"She's on break. Out back."

Gloria topped off my coffee and left. I threw money for the Hungry Man down and added a nice hefty tip, then hurried out the door and around the back of the restaurant where I spotted a large tangle of blond hair and a steady plume of smoke.

"Michelle?" I said.

She turned to me and I got a good look at her. Fine features, hidden beneath some thick makeup. Pretty green eyes. A slight overbite. I had to admit, these Ram's Horn waitresses were kind of cute.

"Uh-huh," she said. Her voice was deep with a hint of rasp. It wasn't the most flattering setting. Michelle stood next to the restaurant's dumpster. I'm glad I hadn't touched the Hungry Man. The smell from the giant green bin of death was overpowering. If I had consumed the 10,000-calorie special, I might be hurling it back up right about now. But the back of the restaurant opened up onto an alley, and there was nowhere else for a smoker to go.

"I'm trying to track down a guy I met . . . his name is Randy, and he said he worked for the salvage shop across the street."

"He ain't workin' there no more," she said. Grammatically challenged, I noted, without judgment. Hey, we all had our faults. Mine happened to be a propensity for lying to waitresses.

"Because of the accident?"

She nodded.

"Did you know him?"

She shrugged her shoulders. "He'd only worked there a week or two, right?"

It was my turn to shrug.

"I knew his boss, Nevada," she said. "He'd been coming here for years."

"Were you guys friends?"

She raised an eyebrow at me while simultaneously taking a deep drag.

"Are you a cop or something?"

"I'm remodeling my kitchen. Randy was going to hook me up with some cool wood for my cabinets."

She gave me a quick glance up and down. *Yep*, I could read her mind, *he looks like Mr. Suburban House-Fixer-Upper.*

"As good a friends as a waitress and customer can be without ever hooking up outside of here," she said, her tawny mane nodding toward the back of the Ram's Horn.

I paused. Not much here, I thought. Then I asked, "Did Nevada ever bring his girlfriend in here?"

She nodded. "Cute girl."

Okay, not much accomplished.

"Randy cracks me up," I said. "I can't believe he still drives around that piece of crap yellow Cadillac. What is it, like, a 1965?"

She shrugged her thin shoulders. "I only seen him in that black Nova. I used to drive one just like it in high school. Mine was gold though. With huge rust spots all over. If I hit a pothole, little chunks would fall off."

"Did you know Nova in Spanish means 'it won't go'?" I said. I was chock full of interesting tidbits like that. It was a big reason waitresses found me so fascinating.

"No shit?" she said. "That's funny."

Our bonding over and with a description of Randy's car, I thanked Michelle, resisting the urge to run my hands through her hair and see if my dog Biffy, who ran away when I was three years old, was hidden in there. He wasn't. I walked back to my Taurus. Well, I had a description of a car. But little else.

I looked at St. Clair Salvage across the street. I wondered if I could just peek in the window and get a look at Hornsby's desk. That wouldn't be a crime, would it? Window shopping? People did it all the time.

They wouldn't send me to Jackson for that, would they?

Nineteen

The direct approach seemed the best. I crossed the
street, went around behind the main building, and pressed
my face up against the nearest window. Through a thin
layer of grime, I saw a lot of open space with a bunch of
gear on the floor. Clearly not the office, although I figured
Nevada Hornsby's corporate décor wasn't exactly
Architectural Digest caliber. I walked down to the next set of
windows. I saw an old desk with a telephone. Okay, now
that could possibly pass as an office. Now what? I really
didn't feel like breaking a window and the law at the same
time. I tried to get a better look but couldn't see directly
beneath the window. I gave the window a hard nudge, but
it was locked into place. Probably more from years and
years of paint as opposed to an actual lock.

I reconsidered the wisdom of trying to get inside.
What were my odds, realistically, of finding a link to the
missing employee? I figured the big wooden drawers in
Hornsby's desk would be crammed with loose papers,
receipts, important documents imprinted with coffee
stains—

"What the fuck are you doing?" The voice shot out
from behind me, and I jumped so hard I felt the Ram's
Horn coffee threaten to slosh its way out of my belly.

"Oh Christ," I said.

My sister smiled at me. "You have the right to remain silent, although with that giant maw of a mouth you have, I've never actually heard you be silent—"

"Jesus Christ, you scared me," I said.

"You were always such a Nervous Nellie," Ellen said. "What are you doing?" Again, she knew exactly what I was doing. My sister was the Queen of Rhetorical Questions.

"All right, I admit," I said. "I'm a peeping Tom. It started with your friend Sue Rogers. She had those giant Eukanubas, and her slumber party you went to—"

"Shut up, John."

"Close my giant maw?"

"Please."

We stood there in awkward silence for a moment. Then Ellen stepped up to the window and took her time looking things over. She turned to me with a raised eyebrow.

"I thought I told you to stay away from this case."

"I am. I just had my daily Ram's Horn breakfast and was walking off the biscuits and sausages—"

"Shut up."

I shrugged my shoulders, deciding to obey her command to keep quiet. I could be a good doggie. *Who's a good boy?*

"So let me guess," she said. "You were trying to be good and not find a way to sneak in and snoop around the deceased's office. Which, of course, would be a severe violation of the law. You'd probably told yourself you'd just peek, deep down knowing it wouldn't satisfy you and that you would have to figure out a clever way to get inside. Spontaneity would take over, and you'd find yourself inside, rummaging around. You might find something, you might not. And then you'd leave and feel terribly guilty, go home, and forget about it the minute you walked through the door and the girls descended on you and made you feel like your coming home was rivaled only by the return of Moses from the mountaintop."

I both admired her and hated her.

I decided to quit being defensive and take the sisterly bull by the horns.

"So I guess you decided to come out here on your own," I said. "Without the assistance of your new friends from St. Clair Shores law enforcement because you wanted to take a good look around yourself, form your own judgments, and keep any discoveries that might impact your case to yourself. And when you saw me, you were secretly relieved because you realized you'd benefit from both my keen insight and my warm companionability."

"It's warm all right," she said. "Like a steaming pile of bullsh—"

"Thank you, I get the idea."

I thought I saw the beginning of a smile play across her face, so I said, "Come on, you know what we need to do."

"No," she said. "Run along, go get a piece of coconut cream pie across the street."

She turned her back on me and walked to the back door of St. Clair Salvage, produced a key, and unlocked the door. She stepped inside, started to close the door on me, but I caught it just before it shut and pushed it back open.

"Come on, don't shut me out," I said. "This is your little brother talking."

She snorted and turned around, ignoring me.

I followed Ellen inside and shut the door behind me.

•

"Reminds me of your room," Ellen said, surveying the piles of junk, empty beer cans, and dartboard hanging askew on the wall. It was funny how even as adults, childhood is never far behind.

I inhaled deeply and said, "Smells like your closet."

The office, if you could call it that, was divided into three rooms. The doorway led into the biggest room where traditionally, the receptionist would sit. Instead of filling the space with a chubby, middle-aged woman with a telephone headset, Nevada Hornsby had chosen instead to furnish the area with a giant rusty anchor. Complete with dried seaweed.

"Very corporate-y," Ellen said.

"Shabby chic, taken to a whole new level," I said.

There were two more rooms, one of them Hornsby's office, the other empty save for a wastebasket stuck in the corner.

Not surprisingly, the rest of the space was filled with giant logs, blocks, and oddly shaped pieces of wood. Most of the wood had at least one side of it finished, in the sense that it had been sanded and varnished. Hornsby's display samples, I assumed.

The wood was beautiful.

"Look at this," I said to Ellen. We both looked at a block of wood that was a dark honey color with some of the most intense grain I'd ever seen before. In fact, it was more than grain. It was swirly almost. It was absolutely beautiful.

All the pieces were unique. Some were dark, almost black. Others were blond. There were some with huge grain patterns, others small and incredibly complex.

"Amazing," Ellen said. "This stuff sat on the bottom of the lake for hundreds of years."

"I wonder if mob informants look this good."

"Why, you wanna make a desk out of one?" Ellen said.

She had stopped just outside the door to Hornsby's office. I could see a few black-and-white photographs hung on the wall. I stepped up next to her and looked. They were archival type photos of early loggers on Lake St. Clair. They showed burly-looking guys in dark wool pants and plaid shirts walking on top of logs with big black boots.

I left Ellen there and went into Hornsby's office. The place had been thoroughly gone over by a forensics team.

His desk was old and ready to fall apart. The chair was old with a smoothly polished seat, made so by years and years of butt cheeks sliding on and off. I sat down and looked around. There was no computer or anything. Just a phone and piles of folders, invoices and coffee cups, soda cans and beer bottles.

It was weird to be sitting in a dead guy's chair, not that Hornsby was the kind of guy who spent a lot of time here. I pictured him on the boat or in the shop.

I used my handkerchief to pull open the drawers. As I suspected, they were chock full of paperwork. I spied a date on one. 1993. If Jessie Barre loved Hornsby, it probably wasn't because of his filing ability.

Ellen had walked into the office and was looking out the small window, which gave a view of the lake. Next to the phone was a pile of yellow Post-it notes, which was interesting because I knew Post-it notes were invented sometime in the 1980s and it surprised me that Hornsby had purchased office supplies that recently. In any event, there were a few Post-its, and I gently pulled them toward me. I peeled off the first one, which was nearly indecipherable. The second was a string of dimensions. The third had a scrawled name and a phone number.

The name was Randy.

I slipped the note into my pocket just as Ellen turned toward me.

"Anything interesting?" she said.

My heart was beating a little quicker than usual. Like I said, I didn't like deceiving my big sister, but sometimes I had to.

"Not to me. Maybe to the Society of Mold and Fungus Collectors."

I wanted to follow up the Randy lead by myself because I figured that it was probably nothing. And even if it were something, I didn't want to put Ellen in harm's way because of some half-cocked idea of mine. Even though she was probably better equipped to handle it. I remembered that one time I had spilled a bunch of milk at the dinner table, and she waited outside for me afterward and kicked my ass. And that was Thanksgiving. Last year.

Ellen took my spot in the desk chair while I looked out the window. The lake was cold and gray, like it so often is at this time of year. I wondered if Nevada Hornsby had ever stood here and contemplated the water. Probably not. He didn't seem like the philosophical type.

I wandered back out into the main room and looked at the different pieces of wood. They were truly spectacular. I'd heard Bill Gates had used this stuff to make the kitchen cabinets in his forty-million-dollar house. I knew that only a guy like Gates could afford the wood.

"All done?" Ellen said when she emerged from Hornsby's office. "Satiated your insufferable curiosity?"

"I guess," I said.

We left, and Ellen locked the door behind us.

"What are you up to now?" she asked. "Going to try to sweet talk a few more waitresses?"

I shrugged my shoulders.

"Why do I get the feeling that you know more than you're telling me?" she said.

"Why do I get the same feeling about you?" I said. "In fact, it seems terribly coincidental that you would just happen to drop by at the same time as me. Are you sure you weren't following me?"

By now we were at her cruiser, and I could see my Taurus across the street.

She climbed behind the wheel and rolled down the window.

"Maybe the next time you thoroughly charm a waitress, you should make sure she doesn't see you cross the street and snoop around a place where a guy worked that you were asking questions about. She might call the cops."

Ellen smiled at me, rolled up the window, and drove off.

I couldn't believe it. Michelle hadn't believed my story. She hadn't trusted me.

I was slipping.

Big time.

Twenty

To a resourceful private investigator—and after a few cups of strong coffee, I had no problem putting myself into that category—there were many ways to take a phone number and match an address to it. If you had a computer handy, there was the Department of Motor Vehicle database, the Nexus database, and even the good old phone directory database. Now, if you were not at a computer, there were still ways to do it. For instance, you could call the operator and say, *I'm looking for Randy Can't-Remember-His-Last-Name, but I've only got his phone number and I know he used to live on Whatever Street.* Most operators will call up the number and say, *Randy Jones?* And you would say, *yep, that's him.* And she would say, *oh, he's not on Whatever Street now, the address listed to that number is 334 Bourbon Street.* You say, *great, thanks,* and hang up.

The problem was it didn't work every time. Some operators were more cynical than others. In fact, they seemed to be getting more and more leery. So when I was in a pinch and I had a phone number but no real name or address, I went to the quickest, most dependable resource I had.

"Nate, I need an address." I could hear the usual hubbub of the *Grosse Pointe News* office in the background. People talking. A copier banging out sheets of stories on the school board, and my overweight friend's heavy breathing.

"How soon and what's it worth?" he said.

"Let me put it this way, I'll wait for it."

He snickered, the sound of a fisherman who's just sunk his treble hook into the lips of a trophy. "It's worth that much?"

I paused. He knew he had me.

"Dinner at the Rattlesnake Club," he said. "With drinks, appetizers, and dessert."

"Oh, come on, that'll cost more than I'll make on this whole case," I protested.

"Okay," he said, putting on his best bartering voice. "I'll limit dessert strictly to sherbet."

"Nuh-uh. Instead of dinner, how about lunch at the Rattlesnake Club? One drink. No appetizers. No dessert."

"Dinner," he said. "One bottle of medium-priced wine, one appetizer, one entrée, and no dessert."

"Lunch," I said. "One glass of wine, one appetizer we split, one entrée each, and no dessert."

I heard him sigh, then he said, "Fine. Shoot."

I gave him the number. He accessed a mysterious software program he had on his computer then came back on the line.

"1114 Sheffield. In the village of Grosse Pointe."

"What's the name?" I said, scratching the address down on the back of a receipt from La Shish restaurant. I think that had been with Nate too. I believed he'd devoured an entire plate of hummus and pita bread before our waitress had returned with our drinks.

"It's registered to a Melissa Stark," he said.

The name meant nothing to me.

"Anything interesting going on, John?" he said. Despite all the shenanigans, Nate was still a reporter, and he actually did work from time to time.

"I'll let you know."

•

The address *1114 Sheffield* turned out to be a small apartment building two blocks from the village of Grosse Pointe. It was one of the few low-income areas of Grosse Pointe. Most people here were renters. A "transitional neighborhood" is how realtors and city councilmen would most likely describe it. There weren't many apartment buildings in the village as it tended to conflict with the image Grosse Pointers try to project. Quaint houses are more the order of the day. But a few apartments managed to infiltrate the market and the mysterious Randy had apparently set up shop at one.

I parked the Taurus and went to the main door which had a little grid with four buttons and four plexiglassed spaces, on which three names were written. The fourth was blank.

I pressed the first button on the list. There was no answer. I tried the second button. According to the nametag, it belonged to an A. Tanikas. A moment later, a voice rattled through the tin speaker.

"Yeah?" A man's voice. Older.

"I'm lookin' for my buddy Randy."

"So?"

"Yeah, he lives here but there's no answer and his nametag is gone. Don't tell me he moved out . . . he owes me ten bucks."

"Talk to the manager."

"Where?"

"See that blue house across the street?"

I turned. Sure enough, there was a little blue bungalow crammed between two apartment buildings.

"Thanks," I said to the speaker, but Mr. Tanikas had already returned to his present activities. I pictured a retired guy doing a crossword puzzle. But who knew, he could have been a senior engineer at Ford, working on a top-secret engine that would revolutionize the auto industry. You had to be careful with assumptions.

I crossed the street and knocked on the blue bungalow's front door. Nice spot if you were a manager of an apartment building. You didn't have to live in the building and listen to the constant squabbles, but you were close enough to keep an eye on things.

The door opened, and I came face to face with the man who possibly held the answers to my questions. He was a small, fine-featured, older man wearing khakis and a cardigan. Imagine Ward Cleaver in his early seventies.

I said, "I'm looking for my buddy Randy. He used to live in one of those apartments over there." I jerked my head toward his apartment building.

"Randy Watkins?" the old man said, and I nearly hugged him. I finally had a last name.

"Yep, that's him," I said.

"Whaddaya mean he doesn't live there anymore? He owes me a month's rent!"

"Well," I said. "I just assumed, what with his nametag gone."

"Aw, fuck," he said, and there went my Ward Cleaver image. "He never wanted his name there. Said he never got any mail anyway. I put one up once, but the stupid bastard just took it down. Waste of ink and paper from my label maker."

Mr. Cleaver narrowed his eyes at me. "Thought you said you were friends."

"Well, he owes me some money-"

I saw Friendly Cardigan Man's eyes slide off my face and look over my shoulder.

I turned around.

A black Nova.

I got a quick look at the driver, and he got a quick look at me, and then he slammed the car into gear and roared around the corner.

Mr. Cleaver said something I couldn't make out, and then I was running for the Taurus. I fired it up, slammed it into gear, and took off after the Nova.

Twenty-one

He had a head start, but it was a small one. Plus, I was no expert on cars, but the old Novas weren't necessarily the fastest cars on the road. And the Taurus, despite its rep as a classically boring, middle-of-the-road, suburban-white-guy car, had a V6 with 230 horsepower. Which I was confident could outgun the old Nova in a test of brute strength.

I gambled that he would head toward Detroit. It made sense. There's a tangible sense of lawlessness in the city. Not enough cops, and really, really bad criminals all over the place. If you're in a car chase, and if you're a criminal yourself, the best place to go is Detroit. There's much less chance you'll ever be found than if you hightail it out to the suburbs.

So I took a chance and headed straight from the village toward I-94, right up Cadieux. I caught up to my friend in the Nova on the entrance ramp. I got on his bumper, and I could make out his head and shoulders. He was a big guy, and judging from the quick glimpse I'd gotten at the apartment building, I was pretty sure I'd never seen him before.

We played cat-and-mouse on the freeway. Randy Watkins had apparently seen every Sylvester Stallone movie ever made because he tried every trick in the book. Using a semi-truck as camouflage. Speeding up, braking down hard. Veering toward an exit ramp, then veering back at the last minute. I tried to get up and get a better look at him, but he always swung back or got behind me. Nevertheless, I did get a few more glimpses, enough to put together my own little "artist's rendering" in my mind. His hair was light brown, almost blond. Thick features. A strong jaw. Kind of a pug nose. Big hands on the Nova's steering wheel.

We dodged each other for a few more minutes until finally Randy made his big move and jumped the shoulder onto an exit ramp. I'd anticipated his move and was already on the exit ramp. So after his poor man's Evel Knievel routine, he ended up right in front of me.

Randy led the way into Detroit proper. I soon found myself in not-so-pleasant neighborhoods. Streets with the requisite cars up on blocks, garbage lying around the street. Lots of Detroit citizens standing around on the sidewalks, hands in their oversized shorts. Looking around, waiting for something to happen. Anything to happen.

I started to worry about what Mr. Watkins' plans might be. It was certainly easier to kill someone in Detroit than it was in Grosse Pointe. And if his behavior was telling me anything, it was telling me that Randy had played a part in the murder of Nevada Hornsby and his deckhand. This was not good news. He may have killed before, which meant he may kill again. And here I was cornering him like a rat in a cage.

As if reading my thoughts, the Nova pin-wheeled into a narrow alley, yours truly a second or two behind him. I flew down the narrow passageway. I could see a big truck maneuvering a garbage dumpster into place.

But no Nova.

I started to brake just as I passed a small opening on my left. I quickly realized I'd made a bad tactical mistake as the rear end of the Nova shot out of the narrow alley I'd just passed. The Nova clipped my rear end, and the Taurus careened into the brick wall. All I heard was screeching metal and the sound of glass breaking. The car rocked to a stop, and I tried to get my bearings. The Taurus had slid around, and I was now facing the way I'd come.

And there, in the middle of the road, was Randy Watkins. Lifting a gun and pointing it at the most obvious direction possible.

I dove for the floor just as the sound of shots ripped through the alley. The shots came fast, one right after another. More glass broke. I heard a ricochet that sounded exactly like it does in the movies. I scrambled along the floor, trying to get to the passenger door. If Randy was coming, I didn't want to get trapped in the car. I found the passenger-side door handle and pulled, but nothing happened. I reached up but it was already unlocked. I pulled the release and threw my weight against the door. Nothing. It wouldn't budge. I panicked, hurling myself against it, over and over again, ignoring the searing pain in my shoulder, my mind screaming at the idea of any moment seeing the pug face of Randy at my window, shooting at me like a fish in a barrel. I kept pounding at the door, finally felt it give, and then I tumbled out onto the pavement.

At the same time, I heard the most beautiful sound of all. Tires squealed, and I nearly wept with joy. I saw the Nova roar out of the end of the alley and around the corner.

My heart was racing, and I suddenly wanted to be sick. I staggered around the car, my legs weak, my shoulder sagging as if I'd knocked it out of alignment.

Steam poured out from underneath the Taurus' hood, and the engine made a bunch of strange popping sounds that could only be the automotive equivalent of a death rattle.

Lights had come on in the alley, and only after a moment or two did I realize they were colored lights. Blue and red. A Detroit cop car nosed its way into the mouth of the alley.

Now I knew why Randy had taken off instead of staying around to finish the job. He'd been able to hear sirens. I hadn't.

I couldn't stand anymore. My legs kind of gave out, and I sat down on the pavement. Another Detroit cop car slid to a stop behind the first one. The driver's door of the first squad car opened and a big guy got out. He held his gun up and pointed at me. Boy, that was the second gun pointed at me in a matter of minutes, and I sure didn't like it.

He slowly walked up to me. Not worried, but not entirely casual either. I imagined he could see the bullet holes in the rear window.

He waited a long moment, almost studying me with a bemused expression. I figured he would tell me to put my hands up, or to get on my stomach on the ground while he frisked me or took a whack at me with a nightstick.

He did neither.

Instead, he spoke to me. And when he did, his voice sounded beyond casual. He sounded bored.

"License and registration," he said.

Twenty-two

"It wasn't a bullet," I said.

"Oh, don't give me that shit," Anna said. I'd gone through the expected ordeal: a statement at the police department in Detroit, several informational interrogations, paperwork up the yin yang, a stop at the emergency room for two stitches on my arm, and now, several hours later, I'd finally come home.

"I'd tell you if I'd been shot," I said. "They taught us that in marriage class. Always tell your partner about gunshot wounds."

"What is it then?" she said, ignoring me. Her tone was high, cynical, and severely pissed off.

"A chunk of metal from the car," I said. The truth was the doctor hadn't been entirely sure. It could have been a fragment from the bullet. A fragment from the windshield. Or, much less likely, a scrape from the car. In all likelihood, I had been shot. I just couldn't admit it to myself. And I sure as hell wasn't about to say it to my wife.

"Shrapnel from the bullet?"

"No, I think it was from the car crashing into the wall," I said. "I always hated that Taurus."

"Good, John, keep making jokes. This is all very funny," Anna said. I was about to respond when the doorbell rang. Anna answered the door, and I heard Ellen's voice. I groaned inwardly.

"Well, if it isn't the Terminator," Ellen said, waltzing into the kitchen. She went to the fridge and grabbed a beer.

"What the fuck is going on here, Ellen?" Anna said. Ellen just shook her head, took a pull from her beer, and looked at me. Anna stopped looking at Ellen and turned to me. With both of them staring at me, I felt like a rotisserie chicken. Skewered and about to be thoroughly roasted.

My wife and my sister. Talk about the proverbial rock and a hard place.

"He was always a terrible driver," Ellen finally said. "In Driver's Ed in high school, I remember when he was out on a country road and the instructor told him to turn, he drove into the cornfield." She started laughing. "And then the teacher, Mr. Darnell, said, 'I meant turn at the intersection up ahead.'" Now Ellen really went off. The good thing was that she was obviously trying to lighten the situation for Anna, not for me. The worst part was that the stupid-ass story was true.

Anna looked like she still wanted to strangle both of us. My sister and I don't have much in common, but dry sarcasm at inopportune times is about the only genetic strain we share.

"What were you thinking, chasing this guy around on your own?" Anna said.

"I couldn't call Ellen. I didn't know anything about the guy," I said. "Hornsby had made an offhand comment about his worker, a guy named Randy, calling in sick. I thought I should follow up, even though I figured it was a waste of time. And if it was a waste of time for me, it sure as hell would have been for her."

"Spoken like a true Grosse Pointe taxpayer," Ellen said. "Very considerate of you, John."

"How was I supposed to know that this Randy guy turned out to be such an asshole?"

"Had you even considered it?" Anna said.

"Well, I think everyone's a potential asshole," I said.

Ellen sort of laughed at that. Anna's heat dial went up a notch.

"Well, it wasn't a total waste of time," Ellen said. "The guy is obviously bad news. Why do you suppose he took such exception with you, John? Other than the obvious."

I looked at her then wondered why the hell I didn't have a beer. Jeez, a guy gets in a gunfight and nobody offers him a beer. I puffed up my chest like a prized rooster and grabbed a beer from the fridge. Before I could twist off the top, Anna snatched the bottle from my hand.

"Doctor's orders," she said. Then she twisted off the cap and took a long drink. A regular Florence Nightingale.

"Why'd he try to kill you, John?" Ellen asked again. As tough as my wife was, when my sister got that tone in her voice, it seemed like even the air in the room started looking for a way out.

"Driving a piece of shit Nova would make me feel pretty murderous too," I said.

Anna slammed her hand down on the counter. Some of her beer sloshed onto the table. "This is not funny!"

"Did you find out anything about Randy Watkins?" I asked Ellen. Right after the Detroit cop had called an ambulance and given me back my license and registration, I'd called her and told her what I knew.

"Ordinarily I wouldn't share information with a loose cannon such as yourself," she said. "But I suppose I can make an exception this time."

"Don't do him any favors," Anna said.

"The Randy Watkins identity is entirely fictitious," Ellen said. "He was renting that apartment month-to-month, and the information he'd provided to the landlord was all bogus. And he always paid his rent in cash."

"The car?"

"We're still checking."

"You should be able to pull the slugs from my car," I said. "Might get something useful."

"Thanks for the tip, Perry Mason." Ellen said. "It is, in fact, on its way to the crime lab."

"So the car's totaled," Anna said.

I nodded.

"Does that mean you'll have to use the minivan?" she said. This was good; we were back to practical matters. Much safer ground.

I shook my head. "As fine and sporty-looking a vehicle as it is, I'll be renting a car. My insurance covers it."

Ellen drained the rest of her beer and set it on the counter by the back door.

"Thanks for the beer," she said. "Anna, when he gets sick or even the tiniest scratch, he turns into the world's biggest baby."

"I know," my dear wife said.

"Just ignore him."

"I will."

Ellen walked by me and punched me on the arm. Yes, *that* arm.

I gave a little yelp.

"See what I mean?" Ellen said.

I glanced over at Anna who took a drink from her beer. I could have been wrong, but it looked like she was laughing.

Twenty-three

"You gotta be kiddin' me," I said.

The Enterprise car rental customer representative, a Bill Gates look-alike circa seventeen years old, sort of smirked and looked out at the waiting room. It was totally empty.

"Sorry, man," he said, a hint of camaraderie in his voice. "I feel for you."

Just outside, another Enterprise employee had just pulled up my rental car.

A Pontiac Sunbird.

White.

And a two-door.

"I can't drive that," I said to the guy. I looked at his nametag: Buddy. "We're getting three more cars this afternoon," he said. "If you can wait—"

"I can't wait, Buddy."

Anna had already dropped me off and left. I'd have to call her and tell her to come back and get me. Jesus Christ. Was I going to tail someone in a white Sunbird?

"Sorry, man, there's nothing I can do," Buddy said. "The last Aztek went out fifteen minutes ago. All I've got left are these white Sunbirds. I've got twelve of them."

"Big surprise," I said.

Buddy handed me the keys, and I had no choice but to take them. He slid a piece of paper across the counter, and I signed away what little pride I had left.

"Take it easy on the ladies," Buddy said, laughing. Everyone's a smartass.

•

Considering everything that had happened—Hornsby's murder, my running and gunning with Randy, etc.— I decided it was time to touch base with my client.

I drove over to Clarence's place and rang the bell. When he opened the door and after we exchanged hellos, he looked over my shoulder at the Sunbird in his driveway.

"Don't worry, it won't be there long enough to affect your property values," I said.

"Is that a Sunbird?" he said.

"I can think of a few other names for it," I said.

"Doesn't seem like your style," he said.

"I drove a Taurus," I said. "Taurus drivers by definition have no style."

He nodded again, silently agreeing that I had no style.

"What happened to the Taurus?" he said.

"That's partially why I came to talk to you," I said.

"Come in, come in," he said. "You want something to drink?"

"Coffee would be great."

I followed Clarence into the kitchen while he poured me a cup. He stood behind the kitchen's island, and I pulled up a stool.

"Have you heard about Nevada Hornsby?" I said.

He sighed. "I just read about it in the paper."

I waited him out.

"I'm not going to lie," he said. "I never liked him, never trusted him, never thought he was right for my daughter. But I'm not happy he's dead. He didn't deserve that." He paused for a second then said, "Were you there?"

"I was."

"Were you—"

"Not bad. Just a little shaken up, I guess." I had a sudden thought that wasn't very pleasant. But a part of me was intrigued by the triangle between Hornsby, Jesse, and Clarence. I waited a beat then said, "Do you mind if I ask where you were when it happened?"

His shoulders slumped a bit, either from disappointment that I was going in this direction, or that overall the chain of events had led to this. "I was at a guitar store in Clinton Township."

"Witnesses?"

He nodded. "I was there pretty much all day, jamming, checking out guitars, giving a few lessons. An old buddy of mine owns the store."

"Okay," I said. I then filled my client in on everything that had happened, from the explosion on Hornsby's boat to my car chase with mysterious Mr. Randy. When I finished, Clarence had gone a bit pale. Imagine Kenny Rogers under the weather.

"Look," he said. "I'm sorry for getting you involved in this. I want you to stop working on it. Clearly, I was wrong, and the last thing I want, the last thing Jesse would have wanted, is for anyone else to get hurt."

"But—"

"But nothing," he said, now pacing around the kitchen. "Let me cut you a check, and we'll be done with it all," he said. He started rummaging through a drawer by the cookie jar that must have held his checkbook.

"Look, you can cut me a check, because frankly, I always love it when people cut me checks," I said. "In fact, cut me two if you want to. But I'm not giving up. Someone tried to kill me. Twice, to be accurate. And it's the same person or people who killed Nevada Hornsby and probably killed your daughter. It's personal now.

Besides, I legally need to have an employer to do some of the things I'm going to do on this case."

"No." He said it with conviction, but I could tell he was mulling it over.

"I'm going to do them anyway," I said. "I'm going to find out who killed your daughter, whether you pay me to or not. Consider me Pandora, and you opened the damn box a few weeks ago."

"I just don't get it," he said.

"Don't get what?"

"Why someone would do this," he said. "What are they after? What are they trying to do?"

"As the saying goes, when I know why, I'll know who," I said. "Or maybe the other way around. Actually, both would work . . . I don't know what I'm saying."

Clarence shoved his hands into the pockets of his jeans. Wranglers, I saw. Definitely country and western. "I thought of something else," he said.

"Okay."

"Jesse was building a guitar. A special guitar."

"I thought all of her guitars were special," I said.

"This one was really special."

"Meaning. . ."

"She told me it was for Shannon Sparrow."

"Ah." That certainly explained it. Shannon Sparrow was one of the hottest singers in the country. Technically, she was country, but had achieved that "crossover" status that record executives loved. Her last CD had sold something like seven gazillion copies.

Best of all, she was a hometown gal. Born and raised in Detroit, Michigan. Actually, if I remembered correctly, she'd been born in Detroit then fled to the suburbs in the '70s with the rest of the scared white people.

"It was going to be her masterpiece," Clarence said. "Shannon was going to play it at her concert next week." I'd heard about the concert. Shannon Sparrow was playing a free concert as her way of saying thanks to her

125

hometown. Anna had said she wanted to go. She and the girls both loved Shannon Sparrow. Frankly, give me Tom Petty and some old Stones stuff. But I was already planning to go. The kids would love it, and it was free, right? What the hell. Maybe I'd get myself a pair of Wrangler's like Clarence and do some line dancing.

There was something in Clarence's face I hadn't seen before. It could have been fear. Or more heartbreak. Or maybe he was lying to me.

"Any reason you forgot to tell me this?" I said.

He held his hands wide. "It wasn't that I had forgotten; I just assumed I would come across the guitar. Jesse told me it was pretty much done."

I remembered seeing various guitars in Jesse's workshop and in her apartment. They'd all looked fairly exotic, the kinds of wood you don't ordinarily see. I wouldn't have recognized anything special about any of them.

"Had she shown it to you?"

He shook his head.

"Then how—"

"She told me about it," he said. "Described the wood. It was the rarest of all the wood she'd ever come across. Worm-eaten, five-hundred-year-old tiger maple. She said the pattern was breathtaking."

"But how could you know for sure?"

"I would know," he said. "Besides, Jesse said she put Shannon's name on it at the bridge on the neck. On that little metal buckle."

"Maybe she hadn't gotten around to that part yet."

"You have to do it to get as far along as she was. So it was done. Plus, she always put the name on the inside of the body as well."

"And you didn't find it?"

He shook his head.

"You looked everywhere?"

He gave me a look that I'd seen a tiger on the Discovery Channel give a springbok just before he killed it. And ate it.

"Did you tell the cops?" I said.

"Not yet."

"You should tell them right away."

"Does it mean anything?"

I stood to go.

"There's only one way to find out."

Twenty-four

The Spook reflected that one of the great things about having worked for the CIA was having access to its infinite supply of handy gadgets. Despite the constant complaining on Capitol Hill regarding lack of budgets and depleted funds, the Spook personally had never seen cutbacks or depleted resources in his area of expertise. In fact, never once had he requested a certain new technology and had it denied due to lack of money.

Take, for instance, the handheld modem and miniature computer screen. The public sector had never seen anything like it—and wouldn't for years—but the Spook had gotten it quite some time ago. It was a true miracle of modern technology. It was about half the size of a normal laptop and weighed next to nothing.

You just got a dial tone on the phone, clamped the circular receptor over the mouthpiece, hit "receive" on the keyboard, and an internal modem automatically connected you to any one of several hundred available clandestine mailboxes via the Internet. The connection itself was encrypted and routed through no fewer than a hundred breakers and transferring stations, making it virtually impossible to find out the original location of the source.

He waited a moment for the connection to establish and instantly an encrypted message arrived, which was then descrambled. The message itself was gibberish unless you knew what it meant. If one were to break the code of the message—a task in and of itself that would require hundreds of man hours—it would have no understandable meaning.

It was the best way for the Spook to communicate with his customers. And it provided the absolute faceless interaction he needed to not just do business but to stay alive.

And, best of all, it had been provided by the government of the United States.

Life was good.

Now at the corner of Gratiot and 6 Mile Road, the Spook used the technology to access his e-mail account. He had twenty-one new messages, all of them junk mail. With every one of his mailboxes, he made sure he got on the list of annoying solicitors who spray the Internet with sales messages like a dog with a dysfunctional bladder. Should certain people decide to take an interest in his account, the spam would make their jobs all that much tougher.

The Spook scanned down the list until he saw the message he was looking for.

It read: *"Thank you for your interest in Midwest Condos, Inc. We're happy that you've arrived and are interested in looking into our offerings. We have an especially nice unit near the Village that suits your needs. Let us know your expected arrival and completion of the enrollment requirements, and you'll qualify for a cash bonus! Units are moving faster than anticipated."*

That's the beauty of junk mail—no one really paid any attention to it. And even if someone were to glance at it, in this case, no one would know what it really meant.

To the Spook, however, it was all very simple. Midwest Condos was his Grosse Pointe client—the same one he'd done some work for a few years ago. And the "unit" near the village was clearly a reference to someone his client had been keeping an eye on from the ordeal a couple years back. His client had decided not to have the

Spook take care of the target as, at the time, it was deemed unnecessary. Now, apparently, that may have changed.

He quickly typed back a response to several messages—again throwing more confusion and red herrings—then clicked on the one from Midwest Condos and wrote: *"Thank you for your message. Will appraise unit as soon as possible and let you know when I've completed my inspection."*

The Spook hit "send," waited a moment, and then unhooked the contraption. He smiled to himself, loving it when clients got nervous. It usually resulted in a bigger paycheck. Besides, he wasn't worried. He'd been keeping an occasional eye on John Rockne, and the man was making progress faster than he'd expected, but in the exact direction he'd steered him. So there was nothing to worry about.

He'd play with him a little longer, make him sweat a little more, and then feed him just enough rope to hang himself.

It was a game the Spook loved to play.

Twenty-five

"I need a phone number," I said into my cell phone. I doubted if I could have looked any more ridiculous. A guy in a white Sunbird talking on a cell phone. I prayed to God nobody recognized me.

"Try information." Nate's voice was tired and more than a little fed up with yet another request from yours truly.

I drove up Cadieux, just a few blocks from the village. "You're my own personal information," I said. "Better than AT&T, although certainly not cheaper."

"Speaking of which, you still owe me lunch at the Rattlesnake Club."

"We'll do lunch and dinner one right after the other," I said. "We'll be so full and bloated, we'll get a jug of antacid tablets from Costco and eat the whole fucking thing."

"I'll take dinner at Sweet Lorraine's." This was a chic restaurant on 12 Mile Road and Woodward.

Much more affordable than the Rattlesnake Club. Nate was backing off, not wanting to push his gravy train too hard. I just wasn't in the mood to appreciate such a magnanimous gesture.

"I want the Thai noodles for an appetizer," he said.

"How about you give me the damn number *before* you give me your frickin' order?"

He sighed. Nothing made him more unhappy than changing the topic of conversation away from food. "What."

"Shannon Sparrow."

"You want an autograph?" he said. "Or do you want to just tell her how her music has changed your life?"

"I'll ask her to sign your ass."

He sighed again. "You're awfully hostile today, John."

I was going to tell him about the car chase and shooting but he'd probably be pissed, and I hadn't called him to give him the story.

"Any idea how I can get a hold of her, Nate?" I said. "I can almost smell Lorraine's Chicken and Shrimp Creole." He said something I couldn't make out, although he did sound happier now that I'd brought the conversation back around to Sweet Lorraine's. I heard another voice in the background.

"Let me call you back," he said.

I thumbed the disconnect button and set the cell phone on the seat next to me.

The village was pretty much deserted, save for the few souls frequenting the Kroger supermarket, Borders bookstore, and Blockbuster. There had been a nice Jacobson's department store anchoring the village, but it went out of business. They were putting in a giant drug store there. Nothing says "distinguished, well-to-do community" like a giant fucking drug store. When it's done, Grosse Pointe will have the highest citizen-to-hemorrhoid cream ratio in the country.

A moment later, my phone rang.

Nate rattled off a phone number, which I scrawled on the back of the La Shish receipt. Christ, I really needed a little notepad or something. One of those goofy, pretentious-as-hell deals with a suction cup that sticks on the dashboard. It's like a giant sign that says, *I'm so full of ideas I need a pad on my dashboard to write them all down!*

"That's her publicist," Nate said, interrupting my Andy Rooney-esque soliloquy. "She arranges all interviews with the media and any interaction with John Q. Publics, such as yourself. She's probably nasty as hell, a guard dog to attack the rabble. Like you."

"She's not going to know what hit her."

"So Rattlesnake Club on Thursday and Sweet Lorraine's on—"

I hung up on him.

It wasn't that I would welch on him, but agreeing to the bribe was a whole lot different than scheduling payment of the bribe. It seemed like the more time I could put between the two, the better business deal it became.

While I drove toward my office, I dialed the number. If what I'd heard about stars and their "people" was true, the woman whose number Nate gave me would be on call twenty-four hours a day, seven days a week.

She answered right away.

I introduced myself, explained I was a private investigator looking into the murder of Jesse Barre and that I would like to ask Ms. Sparrow a few questions, preferably face-to-face.

"Hmm," she said. "She's so busy now that she's home. Is this a police matter?"

"No, like I said, I'm a private investigator."

"I really don't think there's a possibility with her schedule . . ."

"It has to do with the guitar that Jesse Barre was building for her," I said. "I have to ask her some very important questions. Questions that, unless I get the chance to ask them, will most likely merit a call to the police so they can ask them. Do you understand?"

The woman at least pretended to give it a moment's thought. I could practically hear the tumblers fall into place just before the safe popped open.

"Is there a number where I can reach you?" she said.

It was a start.

In the time I waited for a call back from Shannon Sparrow's "people," I got back to my office and checked messages. There was one from Anna reminding me she had book club tonight. They were reading *The Good Earth* by Pearl Buck. I'd read it in college for a comparative literature class. All I remember was a brutal scene where a Chinese peasant woman gave birth alone in a room, cleaned herself up, then made dinner for her husband. I could picture the fun I'd have giving the book club my view on that scene. I'd never make it out of there alive.

I opened some mail, leafed through a *Bow Hunter* magazine that the post office kept delivering for the tenant who'd left this space years ago.

Just as I was really getting into an article debating the merits of compound bows reinforced with titanium, my cell phone rang.

"Yeah?" I asked, seeing the number and not recognizing it.

"This is Molly Lehring, returning your call." Shannon Sparrow's assistant had a voice that was the epitome of crisp, cool professionalism. She gave off as much warmth as a meat freezer.

"Uh-huh," I said.

"Shannon can meet with you in exactly one half hour. She has about a twenty-minute window in her schedule."

"What a coincidence," I said. "I, too, have a twenty-minute window in my schedule. Let's do it!"

There was dead silence as the woman on the other end let me know that there was no time for levity in Shannon Sparrow's busy world.

I started to give a more official acceptance of the offer, but then realized that this woman wasn't seeking it.

"Where are you currently located?" I said, sounding like the very textbook definition of professionalism.

"Eight Four Zero Lake Shore Drive. Grosse Pointe Shores."

"I'll be—"

She interrupted me with a quick disconnection. Now that didn't seem professional to me. Apparently, Molly Lehring skipped the class on public relations.

I checked the number on my cell phone then programmed it into my phone's memory. I figured if I ever got bored, I'd use it to bug the living shit out of Ms Lehring.

Twenty-six

I pulled into the driveway of a monstrous Grosse Pointe, Lakeshore Drive mansion. It looked like a medieval fort with at least three or four turrets and massively thick beams. Brick, slate roof, a couple sets of guest cottages. Easily worth seven figures, probably eight.

There was no doubt in my mind that the house had not seen many white Pontiac Sunbirds coming up the drive. I parked the car with no small amount of pride and rang the quaint little doorbell, at the same time noticing the high-tech security cameras trained on me. They were recessed tastefully, but they were there.

The man who answered the door was actually a woman, once I looked more closely. She had a crew cut and wore a short-sleeved polo shirt exposing extremely impressive biceps and forearms, at the end of which dangled two meaty, veiny hands. Picture Ernest Borgnine after a gender reassignment that never really took.

"John Rockne," I said.

"Ah yes, I was told you'd be arriving shortly." Her voice was worthy of a barbershop quartet. She'd have the baritone's part.

Even though she'd been expecting me, she produced a clipboard, scanned down, then nodded her ham-hock head to let me know all the requisite paperwork was in order.

"My name's Freda," she said.

"Lovely," I said.

Sans a visible expression, she stepped aside, and I caught the scent of either Aqua Velva or Hai Karate.

"This is Erma," she said and lifted her Kirk Douglas chin toward the hall. Freda's twin stepped out from a doorway and nodded to me.

"Hey, Erma," I said. I sounded nice and chipper. If anything, she was more muscular than Freda. Either one could crack my head like a walnut. Erma wore a sport coat, and among her many bulges, I noticed one in particular underneath her left arm. It would probably be a big-caliber gun. You had forearms the size of Dubuque hams, you needed the opportunity to put them to use.

I walked down the hall between them, feeling like the special sauce between two all-beef patties.

The matching Bronko Nagurskis showed me to a small office where a bone-thin woman with wispy brown hair, rosy cheeks, and a small mouth with small white teeth was talking on a cell phone. She sat behind a small glass desk, her black-nylon-encased legs crossed. A white laptop was open in front of her. While she talked, her eyes scanned the computer screen.

Her fingers tapped hard on the keyboard, twice, and then said into the phone, "They're your fucking problem now."

She paused, glanced at me, then looked back at the screen.

"You were paid to do a job, not fuck up," she said. "Fix it and don't call me until you do." Her voice was as sharp and cutting as the points of her high heels.

She disconnected the call and looked at me.

"John Rockne," I said.

"She's in the studio." The way she said it, it sounded like I was interrupting Shannon Sparrow in the middle of taking a crap.

"I'm sure it won't take long," I said. "By the way, are you Molly?"

137

She ignored me and my outstretched hand, then answered the phone after it vibrated on the desk.

"Are you sure?" she said, her voice softer, almost warm. Something told me the boss was on the other end of the line. There was a brief pause before she locked her eyes onto mine.

"I'll bring him right up," she said.

•

The first thing I saw of Shannon Sparrow in person was her pubic hair.

"Shannon, this is Mr. Rockne," Molly said, and immediately took her leave.

The famous singer sat spread-eagled in an overstuffed armchair, wearing a sports bra and a pair of bikini underwear rolled down to just above her happy place. I stood there, open-mouthed, God only knows what kind of expression on my face. I didn't know what to say. "I'm your biggest fan" didn't seem right under the circumstances. Nor did "I really admire your work."

She pressed a wet washcloth against her pubic mound, and then with a straight razor, she sheared about a half-inch off the top of her patch, as it were. She then lifted the razor and with a finger, delicately brushed the pubic hair into an envelope.

"Is this a bad time?" I said, thinking this was a really bad time for me. Maybe when I was young and single it would have been fun, but a happily married man, even if he is a private investigator, didn't really need to be seeing something like this.

"I send them to my doctor for analysis," she said, by way of greeting. So I guess she didn't think it was a bad time. "You know, they study my vitamins, nutrients, what I'm missing, what I've got too much of."

"I never realized you could learn so much from pubic hair," I said. And I'd just used "learn" and "pubic hair" in the same sentence.

"It's like Nietzsche said, 'when you look into pubic hair, pubic hair looks into you,'" she said. She gave a weird sort of giggle after she said it.

"Well, I suppose in your job you have to be very aware of your health," I said. I felt like I was trying to communicate with an alien. I needed Richard Dreyfuss to start playing notes on an organ.

Shannon Sparrow took the opportunity to respond by producing a huge joint. She took a monstrous hit from it. She then set the joint back in an ashtray, picked up the razor, and sheared off another half inch of pubic hair. It was like she was trimming the shrubs.

"Do you mind if I ask you a question or two?" I said.

"Shoot," she said and shook off another batch of clippings into the envelope.

"Jesse Barre."

"Technically that's a statement," she said.

"Let me rephrase. What do you know about Jesse Barre?"

"So sad," she said, without a trace of emotion in her voice. She lifted the joint and gave it a good two-second suck. Maybe that was how she grieved. Boy, I had enough to go to the tabloids. I wondered what the *National Enquirer* would pay. I could see the headline: P.I. Claims Famous Singer Shaves Pubic Hair while Smoking Marijuana!!!

"How well did you know her?" I said.

"We bumped into each other once in a while," she said. "Well, when I wasn't traveling. You know her dad right? You're working for him?"

I smiled. "I don't remember telling you that."

She shrugged her shoulders. "Someone did."

The stench of the marijuana smoke was getting to me. Or maybe it was the little scene unfolding in front of me.

Probably both. I felt like I was stuck in some kind of 1960s experimental film and soon a man in all black with a long goatee would come out and start rambling about the symbolic roots of fascism.

"Tell me about the guitar she was making for you."

"Oh, Christ, I'd practically forgotten about it," she said. She shook her head, a vaguely self-condemning act. "I've got quite a few, but this one was going to be special. Jesse said she was making it just for me—you know, my size, my playing style, my sound, as it were."

"Did you approach her or did she approach you?"

She sucked on the joint then answered while exhaling. "I approached her. I'd seen a lot of her guitars around. Studio guys love to record them. A lot of dumbasses think they're only for looks, but the sound is truly incredible."

"So you asked her to—"

"I told her to spare no expense," she said. "I just wanted her to make her masterpiece. She told me she loved it so much, you know.

"The guitar?"

"*Building* guitars. It was what she lived for." Now, for the first time, some emotion crept into Shannon's voice. She and Jesse had obviously enjoyed some sort of relationship. How deep it had gone, I wasn't sure.

"I guess in that sense, she died happy, doing what she loved to do," Shannon said. "We should all be so lucky."

She licked the envelope and sealed it closed, then rolled her panties back up. What, no aftershave lotion?

"If she had finished it, how much do you think a guitar like that would have been worth?" I said.

"Fifty grand. A hundred grand," she said. "More if I'd actually played it." No boastfulness on her part, just a statement of fact.

"Do you know if she finished it?" I said. "Do you have it?"

"Nope. She must have been close to finishing it. I was going to play it at the concert, which is just a week or so away. But I never got it."

"She never contacted you and told you it was ready?"

"No, she didn't work that way. You didn't rush Jesse. She did what she did, and she told you when it was ready."

"If she loved building guitars so much, why do you think she was going to take a sabbatical?" I said, using the word Nevada Hornsby had used.

The joint stopped halfway to her mouth. "Sabbatical? What sabbatical?"

I shrugged. "Someone told me she was maybe going to take some time off from her work. Do something else."

Shannon inhaled a few cubic feet of pot smoke. "Not Jesse. She couldn't stop building guitars any easier than Van Gogh could have stopped painting. I think it was more than a passion, it was her calling in life."

She took another hit. Her eyes were bloodshot and I felt a little faint.

"Thanks for your time," I said. "How did you find out about her death?"

"My manager." I waited, thinking maybe she'd like to add thoughts about her reaction, but nothing happened.

"Can I call if I have any more questions?" I said.

"You have Molly's number?"

"Yeah."

"Sure. Anytime. You coming to the concert?"

"You bet," I said.

"I'll have Molly give you a backstage pass," she said. "Do you have kids?"

"Two of the biggest Shannon Sparrow fans in the world," I said. It was a little bit of a lie. They actually liked the Dixie Chicks a lot more, but brutal honesty wasn't needed right now.

"I'll have Molly hook you up. I try to make the shows good for families, you know. Some of my biggest fans are young kids."

I was sure her pubic mound was raw and angry, and my eyes were dry and irritated from the marijuana, but damn if she wasn't making herself sound like the poster girl for family fun.

"Okay, thank you," I said. "But I guess I do have one more question. How often do you have to . . . shave?"

"It's kind of when I feel like it." She scowled, looking down at her crotch. "This is always the tough part."

"You should borrow some Aqua Velva from Freda," I said.

"Who's Freda?"

I left then, Shannon reaching for the joint, me gasping for fresh air.

Twenty-seven

Molly instantly appeared and produced four backstage passes as if she'd been present during my conversation with Shannon. Maybe she had.

"She seems very normal and down to earth," I said. I thought I saw a little smile creep onto Molly's face. New in the self-help section of your local bookstore: *Building Better Relationships through Sarcasm* by John Rockne.

She walked me all the way to the front door without saying a word. Then just as she was about to show me out, her pager went off.

"Hold on," she said to me. She flipped open a cell phone and listened for a moment, then snapped it back closed.

"Teddy wants to see you," she said.

"Who——?" I started to ask, but she'd already turned on her heel and was headed back into the house. *Thanks for asking*, I thought. *Why yes, I do have time to chat with someone else.*

I caught up to her just as we entered what would normally be considered a library. Floor-to-ceiling bookshelves, made of some dark wood, like cherry or mahogany, surrounded the place and matched the dark wood trim throughout the room.

But under these circumstances, it wasn't a study. It looked like some kind of slinky private room at a nightclub.

Chairs and sofas were scattered around, filled with what I assumed could euphemistically be described as "Shannon's people." There were probably about twenty of them all together. They were sort of an odd mixture. A few looked like New York runway models, some refugees from the 1970s, others prim and proper Wall Street types.

Now I knew where the term *hangers-on* came from. Maybe it should be changed to *hangers-around*. Because if there were ever a group of people who looked like they had no place to go, no job to do, not a care in the world, it was this group. Most of them were drinking. Beer, wine, cocktails. You name it. Same with the smoking. Cigarettes, cigars, joints, maybe even a crack pipe somewhere.

I wondered if they had business cards that simply said *Professional Leech.*

Music blared from some kind of sound system whose camouflage rendered it completely invisible. Not that it mattered, because guitars were being strummed, clashing with the music as well as with each other.

Of course, I shouldn't have rushed to judgment. Maybe it was a high-powered business meeting. In fact, that thought led me to the man who appeared to be in charge.

He was seated in front of, rather than behind, a massive desk. He had a shaved head, a nice tan, and blue eyes. He reminded me of a college football coach. This, I assumed, was Teddy. And, listening to my private investigator's hunch, I had a pretty good idea he would turn out to be Shannon's agent or manager: PI talks to big star, manager wants to know why.

The suit he had on looked expensive. Fifteen percent of whatever Shannon Sparrow grossed was probably a pretty respectable annual take. Maybe five or ten million?

He held a black cane over his knee. He smiled at me. His teeth were straight and a brilliant white. Behold the power of bleach.

I turned, expecting Molly to do the instructions, but she'd already left. I admired her footwork. Doug Henning couldn't have made her disappear any faster.

"The PI," he said. His voice was as smooth as his bald dome. If anyone noticed my arrival, they all hid it carefully. It seemed a safe bet that the stuff they were drinking and smoking held a lot more interest than I did.

"The manager," I said.

He smiled. "Molly told you."

"No."

"Then . . ."

"Who else would you be? A roadie?"

Again, a light, self-mocking laugh. He held out his hands and gave a little clap. Like I was a seal who'd just jumped through a hoop at Sea World. "Good point. I'm Teddy Armbruster."

"John Rockne," I said.

He folded his arms and watched me for a moment. I sensed it was going to be one of those little power-struggle games. Make the uninitiated feel uncomfortable.

"Well, if that's all you wanted," I said and turned back toward the door.

"John," he said.

I turned back. "Look, Teddy, I've really got to get going. Can you cut the dramatic power bullshit and tell me what you want?"

A few of the bloodsuckers lifted their heads up. It seemed that challenging Mr. Armbruster wasn't the typical modus operandi.

"You're direct," he said. "I like that."

He fixed those baby blues on me and said, "Did you get all of your questions answered? With Shannon?"

"For now," I said.

"See, that's why I wanted to talk to you," he said. He set the cane on the desk behind him and folded his arms across his chest. It was quite a feat. Both his arms and his chest were pretty thick. I bet he had a Bowflex on his private plane.

Teddy said, "Shannon has to concentrate on the concert, which is only a week away. It's a big deal, back home in front of all her friends. That's a lot of pressure."

"She's used to it by now, isn't she?" I said.

"As well as a million other things," he continued, ignoring my question. "I thought it would be good for you to get these questions in, but from here on out, maybe you should run them by Molly who'll run them by me first, and then at the appropriate time, I'll talk to Shannon."

He *was* a college football coach, I thought. He'd just diagrammed a perfect case of running interference. Or the famous end-around.

"I know it's your job to make your client's life easier," I said. "But I have a client too. And it's my job to find out who bashed his daughter's head in. So I'll take your request into consideration, but let's not forget where it falls in terms of priority, okay?"

By now, all the hangers-on were looking at me. I watched them back. One in particular, a woman in a white silk blouse and red velvet pants, walked over to me.

"Why don't you stay and have a drink?" she said.

"Memphis," Teddy said, a stern warning. "I'm sure Mr. Rockne has better things to do."

The woman held out her hand. "Memphis Bornais. I'm Shannon's songwriter."

I took her hand. "John Rockne, private investigator."

"Come along, Mr. Rockne," I heard a voice say behind me. Molly had reappeared.

"Thanks again, Mr. Rockne," Teddy said. "I've enjoyed your directness." Teddy smiled, nodded his head like he'd enjoyed the fuck out of my company. "You don't hesitate either. I really like that."

Without hesitation, I said, "Plenty more where that came from."

•

I went back to the office and worked the phones. Oddly enough, my mind wasn't on the case, despite the unsettling meetings with Shannon Sparrow and her slimeball manager.

I decided to call Clarence Barre. He wasn't home, but I left a message telling him I wanted to ask him a few questions about how well he knew, and how well Jesse knew, Shannon Sparrow.

My last call went to Nate. I wanted to ask him what he knew about Shannon Sparrow and her entourage. Nate had an encyclopedic knowledge of local history. He knew anyone and everyone that ever had a significant connection with Detroit.

And on the unlikely occasion in which he didn't know the answer or answers, he could almost always point me in the direction of someone who did.

But I'd be goddamned if I was going to commit to another meal. At this point, I could be labeled an "enabler" by a psychologist. I felt like Nate was a drunk, and as long as he kept helping me, I kept buying him shopping carts full of Budweiser. I'd have to figure something else out.

I punched in his number on my phone.

"I was just about to call you," he said. I could hear background voices, maybe even a siren.

"What, were you going to dicker with me over whether or not an apéritif could technically be considered dessert?"

"No," he said. "And it obviously isn't a dessert as it's consumed *before* a meal. Jesus, haven't you learned anything?"

"Yeah, I now know the difference between pâté and a patty melt."

He ignored me and said, "Where the hell have you been?" This time, I definitely heard a siren.

"Data entry. It's a part-time job I had to take in order to pay for your restaurant expenses," I said. "I get three cents a word."

"Good, don't be afraid to work extra hours."

"Thanks for the advice. Where are you, by the way?"

"Hey, have you talked to your sister lately?" he said.

"Define lately."

"Like . . . today?"

"No," I said, wishing he'd get to the point. "Nate, where are you? What's going on?"

He laughed, a low, deep chuckle, obviously relishing the news. What reporter doesn't love breaking a story?

"Once again, she's proven why she's chief of police," he said.

"How so?"

"She found him."

"Who?"

"The guy."

"What guy, Nate?" I was already on my feet, grabbing my car keys and heading for the door when he gave me the news.

"Ellen found the guy who killed Jesse Barre."

Twenty-eight

It was about as bad as Grosse Pointe gets: a third floor walk-up facing Alter, the street that divides my fair city and the urban decay that is Detroit proper. I don't say that with any degree of snobbishness; that's just the way it is. In fact, the average Grosse Pointer would love nothing more than to have a thriving, vibrant city next to its borders. But that wouldn't be happening any time soon. For now, it was duck pâté on one side, duck-for-cover on the other.

The building itself was an ugly structure that probably hadn't met a housing code since Nixon took office. You certainly wouldn't find it on any of the brochures at the Grosse Pointe Hospitality Center.

The coroner's van was already outside.

I parked the lovely white Sunbird right out on the street. I sort of hoped someone would steal it—that way I could share the embarrassment a little bit.

I climbed the steps and walked inside, where I saw my sister standing in the doorway. She had her hand on the butt of her gun and was watching the coroner and crime scene technicians doing their thing. She turned to me as I got to the top of the rickety steps.

"What's a nice girl like you doing in a place like this?" she said. No place was sacred when it came to my sister giving me crap.

"Your buddy Nate call you?" she said. Ellen lifted her chin, and I saw him outside, talking on a cell phone. He was eating what looked to be a corndog. I looked around to identify the possible source of the corndog, maybe a diner or something. Nothing. You had to admit, the guy was pretty impressive.

"My instincts brought me here," I told her.

"Your instincts are about as sharp as the vic's," she said, and gestured toward the inside of the house. She walked off in that direction, and I followed. She hadn't invited me to tag along but she wasn't telling me to take a hike, either. I wasn't sure why she put up with me. On good days, I believed she liked having me around to watch her back. On bad days, I was certain she did it for me out of pity. The successful sister, chief of police, pitying her disgraced, deadbeat PI brother. The duty of the sister just as important as the duty of the law. Maybe there was a little bit of both in her reasoning to let me hang out. I doubted I would ever know. I sure as hell knew Ellen wouldn't tell.

I followed her deeper into the apartment. I wouldn't have imagined it possible for the inside of this place to look worse than the outside, but that was the case. The smell was bad, of course. My sense of smell, always reasonably astute, told me that the death hadn't happened terribly recently. Maybe not long after Jesse Barre had been killed.

We got to the doorway to the living room, and I said to Ellen, "Who is the vic, by the way?"

She stopped outside the room where crime scene technicians were finishing up. Flashbulbs were still popping. I saw fingerprint dust spread all around, and the coroner was in the process of removing the body.

"His name was Rufus Coltraine," she said.

"Never heard of him."

"Released from Jackson a few months ago." Jackson, as in Jackson State Prison.

"What had he been in for?" I said.

"Armed robbery. Assault. Attempted murder."

"Nice guy."

"See what's over in the corner?" she said. I stepped past her. There, propped up against the wall, was an astonishingly beautiful guitar.

A Jesse Barre Special. I knew it instantly. The incredible grain of the wood. The styling of the frets, the craftsmanship that was so apparent in every wormholed inch of the thing.

"How'd he die?" I said.

"Nobody taught him portion control."

Ellen didn't have to give me her version of what had happened—it was obvious. The recently released Mr. Coltraine, like so many convicts unable to adjust to life outside, instantly reverted to his criminal past and went on the prowl. He spotted a lone woman working late at night, and he broke in and gave her a little bit of what he learned in prison. So he killed Jesse Barre. A crime of opportunity. Mr. Coltraine snatched a couple of guitars, bought some crack or heroin or whatever he was into to celebrate, and had just a little too much of a celebratory toot.

End of story.

I looked over the scene before me in the living room. It was a dump in every sense of the word. Stains on the floor, holes punched in the drywall.

Apparently Mr. Coltraine had fallen off the rickety, gutted couch onto the living room floor. Truly a party gone bad. Plastic baggies, spoons, and other paraphernalia were carefully marked on the floor.

And a couple feet away was a guitar. My sister walked over to it, stepping carefully. I followed suit until we both stood over it, looking down.

It was a beauty, all right. The wood had a grain I'd never seen before. Almost like a sixties rock concert poster, full of weird vibes and deep patterns you could almost fall into. It was beautiful. A work of art.

"Can you say, 'Case closed'?" Ellen said.

I looked at the guitar again, this time more closely. I had learned a little bit on my studies when I took the case. I recognized the incredible grain of the wood, naturally. I recognized the grain and styling of the neck as well. The bridge. The pick guard. And I knew what the fancy stuff was.

However, there was one giant flaw in the guitar.

I didn't see Shannon Sparrow's name on it.

I remembered what Clarence Barre had told me about the guitar Jesse was building for Shannon Sparrow. He had said that Jesse put a little brass piece of metal somewhere near the top that bore Shannon Sparrow's name. Like the one on B.B. King's guitar that says "Lucille." I saw no such mark.

I looked at my sister.

"Something's not right," I said.

The other people in the room, the crime scene technicians and a few fellow officers, didn't really stop, but it seemed to me that things got a bit quieter.

"What did you say?" Ellen asked me.

"My client told me that Jesse had built a guitar for Shannon Sparrow," I said. "It was her masterpiece. She was making it for Shannon to play at the free concert she's putting on here in Grosse Pointe. With Clarence Barre's help, I've looked for it everywhere. It's gone. It *had* to have been stolen during the robbery. And this guitar isn't it. Her father described it to me—"

"How did he know?" Ellen interrupted me. "Did he see it?"

"I don't know. She might have told him about it."

"So he didn't actually see the guitar himself?"

I turned to her. "Look, Ellen. I don't know what he saw or didn't see. All I'm telling you—"

"You're not telling me anything. And you know why? Because you don't know anything. Come back and talk to me when you do."

That's thing about my sister. She's as stubborn and pigheaded as anyone. She'd pieced together what happened. She was going to clear the case and wasn't ready to look at a different viewpoint. Which was fine. It was that single-minded, tenacious approach to things that had made her a success. But maybe once she'd had a chance to settle down, she'd be more receptive to alternate theories. Doubtful, but I am a highly positive man. The Norman Vincent Fucking Peale of Private Investigators. That would look *great* on my business card. Note to self.

She turned back to me. "Look, even if it isn't the guitar, who cares? So Rufus here stole two guitars, sold one, took the money, and got high. He kept the other one for a rainy day. Unfortunately, the drugs were too good, and he never got around to selling his nest egg."

I nodded. "Sure," I said. Here was where I should tuck tail. Pick it up again later. Of course, I never follow my own good advice.

"You have to admit, though, ol' Rufus might have had a little trouble selling a highly recognizable guitar like a Jesse Barre Special to anyone."

"Yeah, fences are usually pretty picky," she said.

"It was, after all, stolen," I said. "If a fence got caught with it, he'd lose his investment. So not anyone would be willing to take it."

"Yes, people dealing with stolen goods are highly risk-averse," she said.

"But let's say he found a fence."

"Which he probably did, if in fact, he had this Shannon Sparrow guitar. Maybe he never took it. You can't prove he did."

"It doesn't matter," I said. "If Rufus Coltraine had stolen two guitars that link him directly to a homicide, and he finds a fence who'll buy them, would he really decide, 'oh, what the heck, I'll keep one'? Even if it means life in prison? For a rainy day?"

"Why are you so sure he sold anything?" she said.

"How the hell else did he get money for that much heroin? The guy was just out of prison."

"Jesus Christ, John, who knows how much money Jesse Barre had on her when she died."

"No way did she have enough to buy that much heroin."

"That's beside the point! You're not making any sense."

"The hell I'm not."

"You're telling me that criminals aren't that stupid?" my sister said. "You're saying that they're too smart to leave evidence lying around? Who are you kidding? There are murderers in prison now because they left their driver's license at the scene of the crime! Armed robbers who kept the video from the surveillance camera so they could watch themselves and show it off to their friends. Prisons are full of guilty criminals who are some of the stupidest fucking people on Earth. Don't build a case by turning Rufus goddamned Coltraine here into a Rhodes scholar."

Now, not only was it quiet in the room, it was pretty much empty. Nobody wanted to get caught in the crossfire. Or catch my sister's verbal shrapnel.

"Ellen—"

"I've got a dead ex-con with a history of breaking and entering as well as assault, with evidence that puts him at the Jesse Barre crime scene. If you want to make up some bullshit to keep the gravy train rolling with Mr. Barre, that's up to you."

It was a low blow, but I let it go. I was used to them from Ellen now. Besides, I knew how she worked. Right now, she was running the scenarios through her mind, trying to figure out any angle. She had to act like that, had to show everyone that she was in charge and that she was doing her job. In her own way, she'd actually encouraged me to continue.

I turned and went back down the stairs.

Twenty-nine

I knew a guy in college who'd been planning on going into law enforcement too. He was a beast of a guy, six feet six inches, nearly 400 pounds. His name was Nick Henderson, and his terribly original nickname was "House." He ended up not being a cop. In fact, he never finished college, never even got his degree because he beat the shit out of some frat boy. The Delta Chi ended up with a fractured skull, and House ended up having all kinds of legal problems. Anyway, he's now a guard at Jackson Federal Prison, located appropriately in Jackson, Michigan, an hour or so west of Detroit. Probably the better place for him than on the suburban streets of America. His brand of justice was perfect for a maximum security prison.

After a few minutes of searching for the number, calling the prison, and getting transferred a couple times, I finally got hold of him.

"House," I said. "It's John Rockne."

There was a brief moment while I could practically hear him searching his mental Rolodex. It sounded a little rusty. Finally, he said, "Hey, man, how ya' doin'?"

His tone was warm enough even though we'd never been really good friends. Still, a guy that size, you never want to make an enemy.

"Good, good. How are you?" I said.

"Drinkin' beer and crackin' skulls, my friend."

"Good times," I said. Good Lord.

He laughed and said, "What's up? You need a job?"

He'd obviously heard about the end of my career a few years back. Apparently he thought my failures had continued. Maybe that was his impression of me from way back then.

"No, I actually wondered if you ever knew an inmate named Rufus Coltraine," I said. "He just turned up dead and may have something to do with a case I'm working on."

"What do you mean you're working on it?" he said.

"I'm a PI."

"Oh." In the background I could hear some shouting and the occasional slam of a metal door. It was beyond me how someone could choose to work at a prison. It was a dirty job, but I guess someone had to do it. And I guess no one was better suited for it than House.

"I can't say I know anything about him, John," he said. "I think he was in Cell Block D, and I spend most of my time down on A and B."

"Do you know anyone who works on D?" I said. "Someone who might talk to me?"

"Hmm. You could try Joe Puhy. He's the guy on D and could probably tell you all about Coltraine. I don't know how much he'll cooperate, but offer to buy him a couple beers. That might do the trick."

"Okay," I said. "How can I get hold of him?"

"I can transfer you if you want."

"All right," I said. "Thanks a bunch, House."

"Sure. Good luck, man. Keep in touch."

"I will," I said, and then I heard a beeping and slight static. After twenty seconds or so, a tired, slightly grizzled voice said, "Puhy."

I introduced myself, told him that House had transferred me to him, told him about the premature ending to Rufus Coltraine's life, and then asked if he knew anything about his former inmate.

"What do you want to know?" he said. With a voice that wasn't exactly Welcome Wagon caliber.

"Did he seem like the kind of guy who would run out and OD as soon as he got out?" I said.

"Who fucking knows what they'll do once they get out?" he said. "Some of the most normal, well-adjusted guys go out and commit a murder just to get back in. Quite a few even kill themselves."

I could see Puhy was a real student of human behavior.

"If you had to guess, Mr. Puhy," I said. "Would overdosing on heroin seem like behavior consistent with Coltraine?"

"Nah, I guess not," Puhy said. "He was into music and that kind of shit. But you never know. They get a taste of freedom, they want to taste a few other things too. I've seen so many guys who'd changed their lives inside, and then a few months later, they're back after going on some kind of drug or violence spree."

"Did anyone ever come and visit him?" I said.

"Not that I know of. He didn't have any pictures of family in his cell," he said. "I think they were in Tennessee or something. I thought that he would go down there when he got out. But I don't think he got any letters that I can recall."

"Anything interesting about the people he hung around with?"

"No, but he was a pretty social guy."

"What kind of music did he play?"

"A mixture. Blues. Rock. Some jazz. He was pretty good."

"Did he play the guitar?"

"How'd you know that?"

"Just a hunch." So Rufus Coltraine was a musician, gets out of prison, kills a woman who makes special guitars, maybe sells one, buys drugs, and overdoses. On the surface, it made a certain kind of sense.

"Yeah, he was pretty serious about the music," Puhy said, warming up slightly to the subject. "I think he had something going on. Like he could do something with it once he got out. But I don't know if that was just a pipe dream or what."

Maybe Rufus felt like he needed a special guitar or two to make his big break. What had Shannon Sparrow said to me, about how well Jesse's guitars recorded?

"Look, I gotta get back to work," Puhy said.

"Do you mind, if I have any more questions, if I call you back?" I said to Mr. Puhy.

Puhy hesitated.

"Maybe we could meet and I'll buy you a few beers," I said.

"No problem," Puhy said. "I'll be around."

I started to say goodbye, but all I heard was the sound of a metal door slamming and then a dial tone.

•

It was rare that a case of mine collided with a case of my sister's. I was usually involved before crimes happened. The husband cheating on the wife. The guy getting disability, going for the bocce championship in Windsor. You get the idea. My sister, on the other hand, showed up after the cheating husband was run over by the cuckolded wife. Or after the guy on disability took a potshot at the insurance investigator.

But when our cases ran together, there were a few benefits. I got to use Ellen's resources, chief among them: computer databases, addresses, phone numbers, and unofficial police approval to bend a few rules. I'd gotten help with parking tickets as well. Free coffee and the occasional donut too.

I parked the white Sunbird in the farthest corner of the police department's parking lot and went inside. Ellen was in one of the briefing rooms, so I waited in her office. She'd told me recently that she missed being on patrol, that it was getting harder and harder to keep in shape considering how much time her ass was planted in the chair. The price of being in upper management, I guess.

There was a police magazine on her desk, and I started reading about the latest weapons. By the time Ellen came in ten minutes later, I was ready to buy an automatic pistol that held seventeen rounds and came with a laser guide and a night scope.

"What do you want?" she said, with all the enthusiasm of a middle-aged man submitting to a prostate exam.

"Big meeting?"

"Big laughs," she said, smirking.

I waited for the punch line.

"That conference room looks out on the parking lot. We saw this middle-aged loser pull up in a white Sunbird. Trying to park as far away as possible to avoid the humiliation. It didn't work."

"It's a rental."

"All this schmuck needed was a bald spot and a gold chain, and we've got a mid-life crisis in full alert."

"If that was a meeting about Rufus Coltraine, I'm mad I wasn't invited," I said, ignoring her delight at my ride. Actually, the more she made fun of me, usually the better her mood. Sometimes, though, it was just the opposite. I wondered if she'd found something out, and more importantly, if she planned on sharing.

"It was, and your invite must've gotten lost in the mail." Her expression resembled newly dried concrete. Flat, emotionless, and no sign of cracks.

"What'd you find out?" I said.

"None of your fucking business, Mister Sunbird."

I waited a moment then said in my most caring, parent voice possible, "Mom and Dad were very clear on the importance of sharing."

She sat down and rubbed her hand over the top of her head. In Ellen's repertoire of tells, this meant she was frustrated.

"All the music stores and pawn shops turned up squat," she said. "No Rufus Coltraine. No Jesse Barre guitar. We even sent emissaries down to fucking Toledo. No dice. If he hawked a guitar, it most likely wasn't around here."

"And if he didn't hawk it," I said, "how'd he get the dope and why was a valuable guitar sitting in his apartment?"

"Twenty bucks buys enough dope for what he had in him," she said. "You don't need a guitar for that."

I didn't rise to the bait. Instead I said, "How'd you get the call on him?"

"Landlord. Neighbor said they saw someone in that apartment doing drugs."

"Which neighbor?"

"Landlord didn't know."

I nodded. "Ever hear that one about the big pink elephant in the room?"

She crossed her eyes at me.

"They say it's like living with an alcoholic who won't admit the problem," I said. "It's like a big pink elephant sitting in the room, but everyone pretends it's not there."

When she saw where I was going, she flushed a little.

"Coltraine was set up," I said. "No one wants to admit it, but he was."

"Prove it," she said.

"That's what I'm doing."

"No, you're speculating."

"Which is the first step in proving something," I pointed out.

"I need evidence."

160

Which meant that maybe Ellen felt something was wrong but didn't want to come out and say it.

"Right now I've got evidence that links Rufus Coltraine to the murder of Jesse Barre," she said. "Maybe he was walking by, saw her in the workshop alone, and did what he felt he had to do. Maybe he killed her and then got high right away, planning to sell the guitar later."

"What about the Shannon Sparrow guitar?" I said. "Where's that?"

She didn't have an answer for that.

Her phone rang, and she picked up the receiver, "Hold on just a second," she said. She grabbed a few sheets of paper and shoved them at me then lifted her chin at the door.

"The Sunbird is calling," she said.

Thirty

My mind was on Jesse Barre. Thoughts about the case were hopping and skittering across my brain like stones skipped across a lake. Rufus Coltraine, aspiring musician, dead from an overdose. The connections started to come fast and furiously. I had a sudden, urgent desire to learn more about Shannon Sparrow. After all, it was her guitar that was missing. She had a link to the deceased. By the nature of her occupation, she had a link to the dead ex-con. And there was something about her and her people that made me want to dig. I don't know if it was the arrogance of her manager, or the seediness of the hangers-on, or maybe just Shannon herself.

I fired up the Internet, and after less than an hour, I'd dragged about fifty articles onto my desktop. I tried to read them in a rough chronological order, and by the time I'd gone through five or six, I started speed reading, passing over the expected redundancies. There were the obvious details: an early gift for music, a great ear, a few important teachers, and breaks along the way.

And then there were a few surprises. Her parents had both died in a plane crash in Mexico a few years before their daughter broke through. There were unsubstantiated rumors of drug use that may or may not have had anything to do with the tragedy.

Shannon had apparently moved on. There had been an early marriage that, according to what I could find, had lasted less than a year. She had been young, probably seventeen or so.

The next twenty articles or so all said the same thing, talking about what kind of makeup she wore, which boy toy she was currently seeing, her inspiration for her latest album. I noticed that not long after she really exploded – when her first hit began to climb the charts and she signed on with powerhouse manager Teddy Armbruster—all the articles started to sound the same. In fact, they'd changed from the more direct, more honest appraisals to a glossy version, highlighting all that was great and grand about Shannon Sparrow.

By the time I was three-quarters of the way through my cyber-stack, I realized I wasn't going to find anything else. I started to drag the whole fucking mess into my trash can, and then I stopped. Maybe if I went back through the articles and information *before* she signed on with slick Mr. Armbruster, there would be something I could uncover. So I trashed the later articles, made a folder for the earlier stuff, and then dug in.

After another half hour of poring over most of the articles I'd already skimmed, I came across a surprise. It was a reference in one article to a different interview Shannon had done. In the current article, Shannon wouldn't talk about it. The reference was to a magazine called *Women on the Rock*.

I immediately searched and found that the magazine was defunct. Still, I wasn't about to give up. I did a search for the individual *Women on the Rock* issue that featured Shannon's controversial interview and found two links. One took me to one of those annoying "page not found 404" messages.

The other one led me to pure gold.

A devoted fan of the magazine had put all the issues online, and I found the one I was looking for. It had each page scanned like microfilm in the library.

Apparently the magazine was for women recovering from domestic violence or abuse of some kind. And the article was really small, just a sidebar interview of sorts, but in the interview Shannon was asked about her first marriage. She said the marriage was stormy, that there was abuse, and that she'd finally found the strength, mainly through her music, to get out of the situation. It was one of the last things she said in the interview that caught my eye. When asked about where her ex-husband was now, Shannon replied, "Where he belongs."

Alarm bells started going off, and I immediately went back to the computer. I did a search under different headings for Shannon Sparrow's ex-husband. Three search engines turned up nothing, but then finally I hit pay dirt.

The article was from the *Free Press*, nearly eight years ago, just before Shannon's career took off. It was a short article, just a few paragraphs:

DETROIT MAN CONVICTED OF ATTEMPTED MURDER

Associated Press—Laurence Grasso, thirty, of Detroit was convicted in Wayne County Circuit Court of first-degree attempted murder, intent to commit bodily harm, and violation of a restraining order. He has been sentenced to thirty-five years in prison. Grasso, married briefly to singer Shannon Sparrow, will be eligible for parole in fifteen to twenty years.

I hit print and soon my printer was spitting out a copy of the article. I went back to the Internet and did a search for Laurence Grasso. I immediately got a hit.

It was again from the *Free Press*, and it was a few weeks after the first article. It contained only one nugget of information, but it was big enough to make me sit back and take a deep breath. The article detailed where Mr. Grasso would be serving his fifteen years.

The same location Rufus Coltraine had called home.

A little place in the country called Jackson State Prison.

Thirty-one

Ellen was in her office when I arrived back at the station. Normally I would have called, seeing as how I had just been there. But I felt this new information merited a back-to-back visit. Besides, I knew my sister absolutely cherished time with her little brother. She couldn't get enough of me. Who was I to deny her of this intense joy created by my presence?

I walked into her office, and she let out an audible groan.

"Christ, you spend more time here than I do," she said.

I filled her in on what I'd found out about Shannon Sparrow—her early marriage and the later exploits of said hubby. I said, "Let's dig up a photo of Mr. Laurence Grasso and see if he's the guy I think he is."

"Have Becky hook you up," she said.

I went back out to the lobby and found the department's resident computer guru. Becky Kensington was a bleached-blond, solidly built woman in her late forties. She had something like eight or nine kids, but I never knew her to look tired or frazzled. I only have two kids, and there are days where I'm looking for a noose and a strong ceiling beam.

"Chief What's-Her-Name wants a file on this guy, Becky," I said, handing her the sheet of info I had on Mr. Grasso.

"So how you been, John?" she said as she took the sheet of paper and led me back to the department's tech center.

"Keepin' busy," I said. "You?"

"All those kids in school, all I see are upper respiratory viruses, colds, sinus infections, and the occasional strep throat," she said. "Our house is a petri dish with a leaky roof."

"Cupboards full of amoxicillin?"

She nodded as she typed.

I watched the screen, anxious, then sensed movement behind me and saw Ellen watching too.

"Turn around," she said, cuffing me not so gently on the back of the head. I was *never* fast enough to duck those.

Becky laughed, and I said, "That's a quick glimpse of my entire childhood."

"The childhood that never ended," Ellen said. We would have kept going, but the computer screen blossomed into a black-and-white mug shot of Mr. Laurence Grasso. He was a sandy-haired, slightly buck-toothed guy with high cheekbones and eyes that looked bored but that would clearly entertain the idea of violence. I compared it to the face I had seen behind the wheel of the black Nova.

"Fuckin-A," I said.

"Spit it out," Ellen said.

"Hello, Randy."

•

Of course, we had no fixed address for Mr. Grasso. I supposed his nickname growing up was Asshole Grasso, which considering my experiences with him, would have been entirely appropriate. Anyway, his last place of residence was vacated. There were no known family members in the area.

The initial search was best left in the hands of the capable police, namely my sister and her counterparts at the St. Clair Shores Police Department, who were leading the Nevada Hornsby investigation.

They would use all their resources to find Grasso and they would be able to do it faster than I could. On the other hand, if they didn't have luck right away, I would have to see what I could do.

Thirty-two

I was by no means a cyber sleuth. I did use the Internet for business, but mostly just e-mail. Lots of e-mail. I scrolled through my mailbox and saw one e-mail, whose subject line asked me if I wanted to see hot, horny housewives in action. I deleted it without opening it.

I cursed myself once again for ordering a sexy outfit for Anna from an adult catalogue because now I was on their e-mail list. Their latest offering was a product called the Fleshlight. It was a masturbatory device for men that looked like a flashlight, but one end was actually . . . well, you get the idea. Clever, but no thanks.

There were several messages on my answering machine from potential customers. I returned their calls, left two messages, and on the third call, I set up a meeting to talk to a woman who had some "concerns" about her husband. This usually meant she was concerned that his knockwurst was making the rounds. And usually it was the right call.

That done, I put my feet up on the desk and clasped my hands behind my head. No word from my sister yet, so I let my mind wander to thoughts of Shannon Sparrow's ex-husband Laurence Grasso. Probably Larry to his friends, though I doubted he had any.

So ol' Mr. Grasso had found the beautiful, young, talented, driven Shannon Sparrow, seduced her, probably controlled her, and then married her. Once she got a little older and a lot smarter, she dumped his genetically shortchanged ass. Free from the steadying influence of someone with a brain, Larry was free to slide into the life of crime for which he was destined. Not too much later, he wound up at the big house—the same house where Rufus Coltraine sat, ten years into his twenty-year sentence for armed robbery and second-degree murder. Rufus was probably playing his guitar in his cell.

I also wondered what their first meeting had been like. Maybe Grasso had tried to shank him. Or Coltraine had saved Grasso from being raped by the brothers. Who knew? The house of detention could apparently make very strange bedfellows.

I picked up the phone, scanned my notes, and called my favorite Jackson State prison guard, Joe Puhy. I wasn't sure if he would talk to me because I'd never come through on the beers I owed him. After several transfers and sitting on hold, he came to the phone. I re-introduced myself, and he remembered who I was. He didn't seem pissed. After my apologies and reassurances that I would take him out for some refreshments, I got to the point.

"Tell me about Laurence Grasso," I said.

There was a soft chuckle then a low whistle.

"Stay away from that one," he said.

"What do you know about him, other than the fact that I should keep my distance?"

"He's a bastard. Nasty. Mean. Crazy."

"Did he know Rufus Coltraine?" I said.

"He sure did. I always wondered about them. They never seemed to fit."

"How so?"

"Rufus was easygoing, laid back; he had his music. Larry was the opposite. A tried-and-true Detroit boy with a chip on his shoulder, something to prove, always looking for trouble," Puhy said. "And he was a sneak too. Any little way to bend a rule, or even just plain ol' break it, Larry was the guy."

"So were the two of them buddies or something?" I said.

He thought about it for a moment. I could almost hear him scratching the stubble on his jaw. "I wouldn't say they were buddies exactly," he said. "More like guys who maybe had something in common in here, but outside, would never hang out."

"Was Grasso into music? Did he play?"

"Not that I know of," Puhy said. This was a mild surprise to me. "He seemed to like Coltraine's music, but he didn't play anything himself. 'Cept probably the skin flute."

Prison humor—it gets me every time.

"So what the hell were they doing together?"

"Talking mostly. Sometimes, just sitting and listening to Coltraine's music."

How quaint, I thought.

"I don't know," Puhy said. "I wish I could tell you more. Maybe I could ask around, see if anyone knows anything. Be like a consultant for you."

Like a bonefish on the flats, I heard the sound of bait hitting the water.

"Would you?" I said. "That would be great—maybe I could come up with a finder's fee or something."

"Don't worry about it," Puhy said in a tone of voice that indicated I should very, very much worry about it.

We said our goodbyes, and I hung up. What a pisser. Two guys with nothing in common hanging out in prison together. Both get out, and one tries to kill me while the other one is being killed and possibly framed for the murder of Jesse Barre. So was it Grasso who killed Jesse? Why? Did he have some score to settle with Coltraine— and was Jesse just in the wrong place at the wrong time? That didn't make sense. After all, Jesse was building a guitar for Grasso's ex-wife. Somehow the two were connected. Maybe Coltraine was in on it with Grasso. Maybe Coltraine really did kill Jesse. Maybe he wanted one of her guitars for recording purposes, knew he couldn't afford one, and killed her for it. And then maybe he stole Shannon's guitar, and Grasso went and ripped off his old prison mate. It didn't sound too convincing. And if I wasn't convinced, I knew Ellen wouldn't be either.

I started to get a headache. Too much thinking did that to me.

Still, the idea that I was closing in, that I was just a connection or two away from cracking this thing, got my blood going. It was time to find Laurence Fucking Grasso. Since my sister hadn't called, I figured she wasn't having any luck.

But I had an idea.

•

I could rule out all the things my sister would be checking on. Past acquaintances. Family. Places of employment. Former landlords. The cops would check out the logical places. Whether or not they would have any luck, I had no idea. So far, Shannon Sparrow's shit-for-brains ex had proven to be crude but effective.

There was really only one place I might have an edge.

And that was the non-logical aspect of the hunt for Laurence Grasso. I tried to put myself in his shoes. I'm out of prison. I'm running around causing the kind of trouble I love to create. It's what I do. For some reason, I'm sticking around. I'm not running off to Canada. So there's still something I need. I've got to stay close but can't go entirely underground.

Where would I be?

My mind grazed over everything I'd learned about Mr. Grasso. I thought back to what Joe Puhy had said, what the police record had shown, and what I knew about him from when he'd chased me and tried to kill me.

I wondered if he would try to go back to Shannon Sparrow. No chance. She wouldn't have anything to do with him at this point in her life. Still, it would have to be pretty powerful for a guy like that. To think he'd once been married to, had slept with, had shared everything with someone who was now a celebrity. Who was now on the covers of half the magazines in the world.

It reminded me of a joke. A guy and Cindy Crawford are stranded on a deserted island. After a long time, they start sleeping together. They do anything and everything, sexually speaking, exhausting all possible positions and breaking every taboo known to man. Finally, one day, Cindy says to the guy, "Whatever you want, whatever your greatest fantasy is, I'll do it." So the guy has her put on a hat and one of his shirts. He then sidles up next to her and whispers, "Dude, I'm sleeping with Cindy Crawford!"

Illustrative of the minds of many men. I had the feeling that Grasso was mean and violent but also arrogant. It made sense he might want to spend a little time gloating over the "good old days."

So where would he go to revel in his past yet still feel safe? I dug around for the stack of articles I'd used to study up on Shannon. After a half hour or so, I finally found the one in which she admitted being abused, where she opened up a little bit about her first marriage.

I skipped down to the section I was interested in. "I met him at a bad time in my life," she said in the article. "I was dancing at this hole called the Lucky Strike."

The name didn't ring a bell with me. It had probably gone through a few dozen name changes since then. But it was obviously a place Grasso had frequented in the past. Why wouldn't he go down there now and see if he could find anyone who might remember Shannon? Maybe buy 'em a beer and start bragging about how he'd bedded the great Shannon Sparrow.

Flimsy, I knew. But there was video of Cuban refugees making it to Miami in boats even less sturdy than my big idea.

What the hell.

I was sure the Lucky Strike would be worth the effort.

•

I didn't consider it any kind of noble statement to say that I'd never been a big fan of strip clubs. Or titty bars, as the boys liked to call them. As a young man, I'd been to my fair share of them. Gotten the ol' boobs-slapped-in-the-face treatment. Nothing high and mighty about it. I still noticed if an attractive woman walked by.

All these lofty thoughts were on my mind when I pulled up against the curb just past the Lucky Strike. As it turned out, the club wasn't actually called the Lucky Strike. There just happened to be a giant plastic Lucky Strikes sign, probably from the '50s or so, hanging above it. It didn't look like the club itself had a name. Like the vast majority of clubs in Detroit, it was located on 8 Mile Road, the great divider between the city of Detroit and the suburbs to the north. It also happened to be a few doors down from a giant Home Depot and a Burger King. Nice. Stick dollar bills in G-strings then swing next door for sandpaper and a bucket of paint, followed by some chicken wings and fries.

I locked up the Sunbird, thinking that only a moron would steal it. But I didn't want to have to walk home just because I'd run up against a thief with no sense of style.

The door was heavy, wooden, and painted red. I pulled it open, worried about the germs that probably coated the handle, having been grasped by a group of men who would buy ten-dollar, watered-down beers for the chance to watch a naked teenager dance. Occupational hazard, I told myself, trying not to think what these guys do with their hands.

Inside was a beautiful marble foyer with a long mahogany bar and waiters in tuxedoes. Kidding, of course. It was actually just what you'd expect. A stage running down the middle of the place with a bar at one end and a curtain at the other. Small groups of tables surrounded the runway, with some chairs right up against it for those fifty-yard-line kind of spots. For the guys who liked to get right in on the action.

There was a girl dancing on the stage. She had on a fishnet body stocking, or what was left of it, anyway. Her breasts poked out of two holes and sat unnaturally high. Judging by the three or four guys who sat watching her, they probably didn't care if they were looking at a plastic surgeon's handiwork. I moved to the end of the room where the bar was and ordered a beer in a bottle. Six bucks. Ah, that good ol' naked-girl surcharge.

When you got right down to it, there were only so many ways to get information from a place like this. You could stake it out over the course of a few days, or even a couple weeks, and try to learn something that way. Or you could have an idea of who your target was ahead of time and watch for him or her. Or you could walk in blindly and start asking questions. You could probably guess which path made sense to me. I didn't have time for a two-week stakeout. And even though I knew who I was after, I didn't think Grasso would be so stupid as to just hang out somewhere in the open.

The dancer was really working her stuff on the stage to the incongruous tune of Olivia Newton-John's "Let's Get Physical." As I watched the fish-netted youngster on stage bend over and grab her ankles, I figured the Australian singer didn't exactly have this kind of imagery in mind when she performed the feisty little ditty.

I hadn't touched my beer and understood immediately that I wouldn't be putting my mouth on anything in this bar, unlike the four-hundred-pound guy waving a dollar bill at the dancer hovering over him.

Before I'd left the police station, I'd made a copy of Grasso's mug shot. I'd had to do it without Ellen noticing, but old habits die hard, and it'd been easy to go around behind her back.

The bartender was a goofy-looking guy. He reminded me of guys I'd gone to high school with that were easygoing and fun, but you knew would never really do much with their lives. I waved him over and showed him the computer printout of Laurence Grasso's mug shot.

"I'm trying to track down a buddy of mine. Larry Grasso. Do you know him?"

Without looking at the picture, he said, "You a cop?"

I shook my head. "Flunked out of the Academy," I said.

He barely glanced at the picture, and I knew what the answer would be. "Never seen him," he said.

"Is there anyone else here I can show the picture to?"

"Why you lookin' for him?"

"I'm a PI," I said. "His sister hired me to find him. Their mother died, and they need to settle the estate. It's not much, but they can't do it until Larry's contacted."

The bartender shrugged his shoulders and walked away. Clearly, I was on my own.

I pushed my beer back and walked around the bar to a door marked with the single word: Office. The bartender watched me and started to say something, but I knocked on the door quickly and when I heard a voice say "Fuck off!" I went right in.

There was a woman behind the desk with big blond hair. I couldn't see her face because it was buried in the crotch of a thin black girl sitting spread eagled on top of the desk.

"Oops," I said.

The black girl scrambled off the desk. The blonde wiped her mouth off on her forearm and stood up. She was a big gal.

I pulled out the picture of Grasso and said, "I'm looking for Larry Grasso. Do you recognize him?"

"Get out," the woman said, and her eyes flickered over my shoulder. I sensed movement behind me and ducked. Something crashed into the door and I pivoted, then reached up and caught the baseball bat under my arm. I swept my left hand up, slamming it into the bartender's elbow, and I heard a satisfying pop. He let go of the bat, yelped a little, and I flipped it around so it was in my hand. I rested it over my shoulder and winked at him. He glared at me, and I used the bat like a cattle prod to herd him into the office, where I could keep an eye on all three of them. I closed the door behind me.

"Boy, you guys have got a real customer service problem," I said.

"Fuck you," the blonde said. The black girl hadn't moved.

I nodded to the black girl, "Employee of the Month, I assume?"

"Very funny," the blonde said. "What do you want?"

"Larry Grasso."

"Never heard of him."

"Wanna think about it?" I said.

"No," the blonde said. "Jesus, I never heard of the guy." She looked at the bartender, and he shook his head. To be honest, I couldn't tell if they were lying or not. Sometimes it's obvious. Sometimes you just don't know.

I thought about it. I could make some more empty threats, or I could just cut my losses and thank God I wasn't wearing a Louisville Slugger tattoo on my temple.

"Thanks for the souvenir," I said, opening the door and stepping out into the club. The same girl was dancing, and the same customers were staring at her. Breathing through their mouths.

I walked outside, feeling a little silly carrying a baseball bat on my shoulder like I was about to start hitting fly balls for outfielder practice. Something told me I wasn't doing this right. Whether or not they knew Grasso was moot. They were clearly the type that didn't want to tell anyone anything. I thought about what I'd done—maybe I should have come up with a better story. I popped the trunk and threw the bat inside. Who knew when it might come in handy?

I backed the Sunbird out of the spot and was about to turn out of the parking lot when I saw a flutter of movement off to my left. I looked. At the back of the building was the skinny black girl, and she was waving at me. I drove around and pulled up next to her. She leaned in.

"I'll tell you where he is for five hundred bucks."

I pulled out my wallet and counted. "I've got three hundred and sixty."

Her face was thin. Her eyes haunted. She was clearly on drugs. Malnourished. Desperate.

I held the money out to her, and when she reached for it, I pulled it back.

"He's in a house on Barrington with a dancer named Ginger," she said. I remembered when Nate gave me the address from the black Nova's registration—it had been in a woman's name. The name wasn't Ginger though. It was something plain like Mindy or Missy. Melissa. That was it. Melissa.

"Is Ginger's real name Melissa?"

She gave me a look like I was certifiable.

"No real names, I get it," I said.

"Do you know the address?" I said. "Roughly?"

Her eyes took on a strange look, and I said, "If you don't know, don't lie."

She nodded then said, "Alls I remember is it's got a front porch with a refrigerator on it."

I handed her the money. She took it, and her face took on a flush, already anticipating the drugs.

"Don't even think of calling them to tell them I'm coming," I said. "Or I'll come back for a refund, do you know what I mean?" Actually, I had no intention of coming back, but I had to at least make an attempt at the tough-guy routine. Sober, she wouldn't buy it. Strung out like she was, she might consider it. Anyone who knew me, of course, would have doubled over with laughter.

She hurried away from the car and darted back into the building through the door. If the big blonde found out she'd given me the information, I was sure she would have her ass. Literally.

But I had a lead.

Thirty-three

Barrington was located on the southern end of Grosse Pointe, bordering Detroit. All the exciting stuff happened down here. You could take your mansions and your yacht clubs and everything else from Grosse Pointe proper, but it was down here in the area they called the Cabbage Patch that all the excitement went down. They called it the Cabbage Patch, by the way, because the homes are so packed together, like, you guessed it, heads of cabbage in a field. Grosse Pointers are *sooo* creative.

At first, when the stripper had told me to look for a porch with a fridge on it, I thought it'd be easy to spot. But now, driving down the shitty street, I see she should've been more specific. Was it a side-by-side? Automatic icemaker? Freezer on the bottom?

Plenty of bikes and chairs and tables and air conditioners and a car bumper and a body (sleeping, I hoped) and plenty of dogs without leashes. Dogs without leashes. Sounded like a punk band.

I finally spotted a house with a lovely avocado-colored Frigidaire on the front porch. I stopped the Sunbird well shy of the house and put it in park, then got out and walked up onto the front porch. The fridge was in worse shape than it looked from the street. There were garbage bags piled inside. There were more garbage bags on the floor of the porch. I saw that quite a few of the plastic bags had jagged holes chewed in them. Rats. Lovely.

The door was cheap and flimsy. Big surprise there. I thought about what to do. Legalities. Options. Should I call Ellen or not? What if she came and the house was an abandoned rathole?

I thought some more and pressed my ear to the door. I didn't hear a thing. I pressed the doorbell but didn't hear any corresponding sound. I pressed it twice more with the same lack of result. So I pounded on the door for a good three or four minutes. Still nothing.

Goddamnit. By now, I was about to piss my pants. I pounded on the door again and noticed that when I hit it really hard, the latch came all the way out from the door. Hmm. I leaned my shoulder into it, and now I could get a thin glimpse of the room. Already, I saw a story formulating in my mind. Indefatigable PI checks out a lead. Walks up the front porch stairs, trips, crashes into the door, which opens up. He "accidentally" finds himself inside the house! Flippin' brilliant!

Excuse in hand, I lowered my shoulder to the crap-ass poplar frame and plowed my way forward. There was a loud pop and a crack, and the door gave way. I stumbled straight into the living room and the working end of a .357, held in the firm, unwavering hand of none other than Laurence Grasso.

"You took long enough you little fucking punk," he said.

•

He'd changed his appearance from his mug shot. Bleached hair, a bleached goatee. But it was the same guy. The same little predatory weasel eyes, coupled now with breath reeking of cheap wine.

"You just keep comin', don't ya?" he said.

"Like a fly with a nose for shit."

He pulled back the hammer on his revolver. If I had to guess from the aroma of his breath, he'd been partaking in a local wine, probably a merlot. A 2003, perhaps.

"You know what a punk is?" he said.

"Kill him and let's go," a woman's voice said from the kitchen. I didn't know what startled me more: the voice or the utter lack of emotion it carried. Unlike me, Grasso paid the advice no attention whatsoever. He was focused on me.

"Let's go," the woman said again. Wherever she was, I couldn't see her. I didn't recognize the voice. The calm authority, the bored indifference in her tone, however, was unmistakable. I was more scared of the person attached to that voice than I was of the ex-convict with the gun pressed to my forehead. Not to say I wasn't scared. Quite the contrary, actually.

Grasso moved around behind me, sliding the muzzle of the gun across my forehead and around my scalp, like he was tracing the line of a bowl to give me a haircut. He stopped behind me, and then I felt his forearm go around my throat. He pressed in against me and either he had a screwdriver in his front pocket or something very bad was going to happen to me.

"I used to fuck guys like you in prison," he said.

"I'm married," I said.

"Goddamnit, we don't have time for this," the woman in the kitchen said. "He probably called the cops already."

I tried to see, leaning forward slightly and looking from the corner of my eye. All I could see was a doorway and a kitchen cabinet and countertop. I heard the sound of a chain lock sliding, then a deadbolt thrown. She was definitely getting ready to leave. I hoped Grasso would follow her example. Quickly.

I craned forward a little more and the left side of my face exploded in pain as Grasso used the barrel of the gun to deliver a karate chop to my face. "Don't worry about her," Grasso said. "Worry about me."

The side of my face was on fire, and I felt blood running down my chin. The gun slid along my scalp again, this time ending up at the very back of my head.

"The cops are on their way," I said. "They know I'd tracked you down. Do you really want another murder on your sheet?"

I was throwing out marshmallows here, I knew. But I was scared to death of dying. I needed to somehow convince him that not killing me was the right way to go.

"It don't fuckin' matter now," Grasso said. He shifted, and I sensed that he was moving the gun to his left hand, which begged the question: what did he need his right hand for?

"Come on, let's go!" the woman called from the kitchen.

"Shut up!" Grasso yelled into my ear. And then I felt something so hideous I froze.

With his free hand, Grasso tried to pull down my pants.

"Mister Nosy Bitch following me around, chasing me, just who the fuck do you think you are?"

"I—"

"Shut up, punk!"

"You've got to be kidding me!" the woman in the kitchen called.

"Nothin' better than a virgin punk ass," Grasso said, and as he yanked on my pants, I grabbed one of his fingers and bent it back until I felt the bone break, which it did with a sickening little crunch.

Grasso screamed in my ear, and then he curled his leg around mine and pushed me forward. He pinned my arms so that I smashed face first into the hardwood floor. I felt something give in my face, and a searing pain ricocheted around inside my skull. Blood was in my mouth.

I felt air on my skin and knew with a panic that it was my ass. Grasso had my pants down.

"Fucking bitch," he breathed into my ear. His breath was hot and fast. I didn't know if it still smelled like wine, I figured my nose was broken.

I heard the sound of Grasso's zipper, then the rustle of fabric as he lifted his shirt to pull down his pants.

A sound came from the front of the house that had a tinny quality to it. It sounded suspiciously similar to a police siren. We all heard it at the same time, and the woman in the kitchen said, "Shit!"

"Motherfucker!" Grasso said. Doors slammed outside, and heavy footsteps pounded up the front walk. I heard a lot of shouting, but everything seemed fuzzy and out of focus. I tried to move, tried to roll, but nothing happened. I had a funny tingling sensation down my spine.

"You fuck," the woman said.

I heard Grasso run to the front door and shout.

"Shit," the woman said, but her voice was further away now. Had she left?

"Just let me—" Grasso started to say, and then there was a loud crashing sound followed by two shots close together. Boom. Boom.

Grasso garbled something, and I heard him drop to the floor just as the walls around me exploded and the gun boomed. A cacophony of sounds greeted my ears. More crashes, shouts, tires screeching, the back door slamming shut, more heavy footsteps.

I rolled as best I could. A stabbing pain raced up my left leg, and then the back door banged open.

A newer tinny sound from the front porch was going strong. A cop's radio. There were running footsteps as I tried to get my bearings and then someone behind me said, "Freeze." *What a stupid thing to say*, I thought.

I desperately wanted to pull my pants up, but at this point, it wasn't worth the risk. Besides, the cops had arrived, probably because a neighbor had seen my dramatic entrance. Compared to the fear of being raped and killed, having a Grosse Pointe cop see my bare fanny was no big deal.

I lay still, my heart beating, the pain in my body building to a crescendo.

And then I heard a voice.

"Not one of your finer moments," my sister said.

Thirty-four

Later, we were standing outside the house on Barrington. I'd given my official statement, been given a quick once-over by the paramedics, and was now ready to receive the wrath of my sibling. Ellen pointed at my leg, which had gotten a basic bandage from Grosse Pointe's finest emergency medical response team. It was a giant Band-Aid.

"So were you shot?" she said.

I shook my head. "It was a sliver from the floor."

"A sliver," she said.

I could tell she was on the verge of either laughing at me or slapping me silly.

"Yeah, it was a sliver," I said. "A big one."

"Only you could be in the middle of a shooting and come out of it with a sliver."

"A big sliver."

"Whatever," she said.

Grasso had already been bagged and tagged. The crime scene technicians were done and gone. Ellen turned to me. "So why don't you tell me how you ended up presenting your ass to Grasso."

"It was some fine detective work, if I say so myself," I said.

"Luring an ex-con with your sweet butt? Isn't that entrapment?"

"Very funny," I said.

"You know, sodomy is illegal in Michigan. I should take you in."

"Nothing happened."

"Not what I hear," she said. "I heard you were caught *in flagrante delicto*. At least, that's what the boys down at the station are probably saying."

"Would you please shut up?"

"Mom would roll over in her grave if she knew you were sleeping with an ex-con," she continued.

"Okay, that's enough."

"Why don't you just tell me what happened," she said.

I filled her in on my questioning the dancer at the Lucky Strike. How one thing had led to another and I'd found myself on Barrington.

I also told her about the woman in the kitchen.

"Never got a look at her?" Ellen asked me.

"Nope."

"Would you recognize her voice?"

"Maybe."

Ellen thought about that for a moment. "The house is clean. Nothing to tie Grasso to anything, from what we could find so far."

"So what were they doing here?"

She shrugged.

"Well at least we know now that Grasso wasn't working alone and that Jesse Barre's murder wasn't just an ordinary robbery gone wrong."

"Don't jump to any conclusions."

"Oh, come on, Ellen. You're not going to pin this all on Grasso, are you?"

"Why don't you let us do our jobs before you start telling me what I'm doing wrong?"

"Okay," I said. "Fair enough."

Ellen looked me over. "Does your wife know what happened?"

"Not yet."

"Why don't you go home and tell her all about it. Stay out of the investigation for a little while."

It was at times like this that I could really tell she was pissed. Apparently I'd overstepped my bounds again. Well, goddamnit, I couldn't help it if every cave I stuck my nose in had a bear inside.

I left the scene of the crime, as it was. And went home to tell my wife that I'd been shot at again.

I hoped it wouldn't ruin dinner.

Thirty-five

Ellen called me at my office the next morning.

"I want you to come and look at something," she said.

"What, is your toilet running again?"

"Like you'd have a fucking clue how to fix it," she said. "I want to get your take on some stuff we found out about Grasso. I have no idea why, but I do."

"I thought you said you wanted me to stay out of the investigation," I said. "I got the definite feeling you'd tired of your favorite sibling."

"You're my only sibling."

"The two have nothing to do with each other."

I listened to Ellen sigh on the other end of the line. It was always fun to know I'd irritated her slightly. Besides, I couldn't just let her get away with telling me one day to fuck off and then the next day welcoming me back. I was getting whiplash from the sudden changes of direction.

"As much as I would like to keep our work separate, the fact is, Grosse Pointe's a small town," she said.

"Especially for an ego like yours," I said.

"Shut up, John."

I complied.

"What I mean is, a small town means that we're bound to cross paths once in a while," she said. "Considering that we work in similar fields."

"Lucky you."

"Besides, you've done some good work on this case, chasing down Grasso and making some connections."

"Was that a compliment? You gotta be kiddin' me," I said. "Who is this? Am I on Candid Camera? Where's Allen Funt?"

"God, do you ever shut your piehole, John?"

"Occasionally," I said. "Usually during the holidays."

"Call it professional courtesy, but I thought you might like the opportunity to see what we've found," she said. "Say no and I'll never be nice to you again."

"When did you start?"

"This is the sound of the phone being placed near the cradle," she said. I actually heard her voice getting softer.

"Wait!" I called.

Now her voice was really distant. "It's also the sound of your private investigator's license failing to be renewed for lack of cooperat—"

"Hold it!" I shouted into the receiver.

Her voice came back on, this time at normal volume.

"Yes?" she said, her voice thick with innocence.

"You fight dirty," I said.

"I fight to win, my friend."

I grabbed a pencil.

"Spill it," I said.

•

Expecting a rat trap, I wasn't disappointed. The deceased Mr. Grasso had on his person at the time of his death several forms of false identification portraying him to be Phillip Carmichael. Through the efficient work of the Grosse Pointe Police Department, an address belonging to the pseudo Mr. Carmichael was discovered. It was over the border from Grosse Pointe into Detroit proper. A fabulous piece of real estate comprised of two abandoned buildings, three abandoned lots, and a whole lot of garbage.

When I arrived, I could see why Grasso had chosen to spend his free time at the stripper's house with a fridge on the porch. At least there *was* a fridge. This place, a single-story, sagging house, was certainly on the condemned list along with a few ten thousand other properties the absentee Detroit government hadn't gotten around to clearing.

Ellen was already inside, another cop waited just outside the front door. I found her in the main room of the house, which held one duct-taped sofa, a couple dead rats, and two worn-out boxes. My sister stood over the boxes.

She pointed at the rats. "Couple of your PI colleagues?"

"Very cute," I said.

Ellen nudged a box with her toe. "Check it out."

I bent down and leafed through the papers inside. There were newspaper articles, letters, pictures, and a few pieces of cheap jewelry.

"Notice what they all have in common?"

I had. They were all about Shannon Sparrow. Pictures of her concerts. Articles about her. Notes from fans. I assumed the necklace and bracelet had once been hers. Even though it was all in a couple of flimsy boxes, they were very organized, and you could tell they'd been labored over. Someone had spent a lot of time studying these things. Obsessing over them, in fact.

"Her number one fan, apparently," she said. "The flame never died out."

I knew where Ellen was going with this.

"So you've got everything you need," I said.

"He was still in love with her. Obsessed with her. Had to have her."

I thought I'd help her along. "He dreamed about her in prison," I said. "Read about the wonderful Jesse Barre guitars and how much Shannon loved them, decided to kill

Jesse, frame his old prison mate, and present the guitar along with himself to Shannon."

Ellen nodded. "In the context of a sociopath, it works."

"Except for the mystery woman," I said.

"Could have been anyone," she said. "A girlfriend. A junkie friend. A neighbor. An innocent in the wrong place at the wrong time."

I shook my head. "You didn't hear the authority in her voice when she told Grasso to just kill me. She's no innocent. There's more to it than Grasso, Ellen."

She shrugged her shoulders. "You may be right. But he's dead. And for now, the case is eventually going to be closed."

"So why bring me here?"

She gave me a look of exasperation, like I was a kid who didn't appreciate a birthday gift. "I thought your client might like to know about this. And on the off chance that Grasso wasn't working alone, and that there might be future violent episodes, you should know about this."

I looked at her. What a load of bullshit. She had stopped doing me favors a long time ago. Unless I was in real physical danger, but even then she would still think about it.

"You want me to keep digging, don't you?" I said. "Not in an official capacity, but you think there's more to it, don't you?"

She raised her eyebrows and placed a hand across her heart. "*Moi?*"

Thirty-six

The star innocently shaving her pubic hair was gone. I found Shannon Sparrow seated at a wrought iron patio table, holding a long-stemmed wine glass with her gently tapered fingers.

I'd tracked her down through Molly, the ambitious personal assistant who'd told me that Shannon was at a "friend's" house. I coaxed the address out of her by telling her that I had information I'd rather tell Shannon than my best friend, the reporter. Personal assistants apparently have a huge phobia regarding the press.

The house was another giant fucking monster along the lake. Made of stone, huge picture windows and a yard worthy of a pair of goal posts.

After being shown in, I was whisked to the rear of the house by a courteous manservant where I found Shannon and her entourage. Even among the group, she stood out. Whether it was her beauty, or the unconscious positioning of the other people around the person of power, I didn't know. But she was clearly the epicenter of the crowd, even if everyone went out of their way to act as if she wasn't.

I looked at Shannon. She seemed more pale than the last time I'd seen her. Her wineglass was huge. A fucking fish bowl set on top of a tiny pencil of glass. It was a dark red, heavy with sediment.

Before I could even get a hello in, Molly arrived with a gray-haired gentlemen in a tasteful, charcoal-colored Armani suit.

"Ah, Mr. Rockne," the man said, extending a tanned hand. I shook it.

"Paul Kerner," he said. "Ms. Sparrow's attorney."

"One of many, I assume," I said.

He laughed. What a polite man. "I'm afraid Ms. Sparrow has nothing to say today."

"Under your orders?"

"The decision was mutual," he said.

Over his shoulder, I saw Shannon catch my eye and then look away. She took a sip of wine. Or was it more of a gulp?

I turned to Mr. Kerner. I have a confession to make. I never really had a problem with attorneys. In fact, I got a lot of clients from their referrals. Sometimes, though, you can spot a pinhead a mile away.

"Don't you think it would be in your client's best interest to shed some light on what's happened?" I said. "It will only help her both in the short- and long-term."

Mr. Kerner pretended to debate the idea.

"I don't think so," he said.

I sensed the twin hulking shadows of the East German weightlifters. I turned and looked into the ham-like countenances of Erma and Freda.

"Mr. Rockne, I believe our business is concluded," Mr. Kerner said.

The entourage was watching. Shannon wasn't. She was now looking into the empty cavern of her wineglass.

"I've got some information about her ex-husband she might be interested in," I said.

This brought Shannon's head up, and an audible gasp from the hangers-on.

The shadows moved in closer.

"Business is concluded," Mr. Kerner said.

"It is time for you to go," said Erma or Freda. I turned to them, surprised that they actually spoke.

"Piss off," I said, sounding like a little kid on the playground who was about to get his ass kicked.

Both bodyguards stepped back from me, always a bad sign. I can't resist putting on a little show for a crowd, but I didn't want to get bitch slapped in front of this many people. There's something to be said for private beatings. They're usually more painful, but much less humiliating. I especially didn't want to take a public thrashing administered by two women, if that was actually their gender.

Erma, or was it Freda, lolled her head to the side, and I heard a bone crunch. I had a feeling the next one to go would be mine.

"Hold it, hold it," a voice said from the back.

I looked over, and Shannon was pouring wine into a glass next to hers.

"Come over here and sit down," she said to me. "You guys leave him alone."

Kerner had already left. I smiled at Erma and Freda. They were clearly not happy.

"We'll hook up later," I said, figuring it just might happen.

•

It was my first pop star party, and to be honest, I was enjoying it. Before long, the place was crowded with people, music played from invisible speakers, and my wine glass was empty, then full, then empty, then full. You get the idea.

And through it all, I talked with Shannon Sparrow.

"Thanks for saving me back there," I said.

"You seem like an honest guy," she said. "Besides, Erma and Freda . . ." She just shook her head.

"How come you stepped in as soon as I mentioned your ex-husband?" The words came out of my mouth a little clumsily. Not only was the wine thick with sediment, it was strong.

"When I think of . . . him . . ." she said, meaning Grasso. "I want to fucking puke. And I don't mean a gentle upchuck. I mean I want to hurl from the depths of my bowels. I want to just gag and gag and gag . . ."

"I get the idea, Shannon," I said.

"He was scum. Pure scum. I was just too young to know it."

"We all make mistakes," I said.

"That was a doozy."

"Most mistakes are," I said. "When did you hear that he'd been killed?"

She just kind of shrugged her shoulders—obviously she never felt like she had to answer questions if she didn't want to.

"He was shot, right?" she said.

"Couple times."

"Were you there?" she said.

"Yep."

Shannon slugged down the rest of her wine, her hand shaking a little as she held the glass. She set the glass down and pulled out a joint from her front pocket. She tilted it toward me, and I shook my head.

I was a regular Boy Scout.

Shannon looked for a light in her pockets but came up empty. A woman appeared next to her—in her hand was a Bic with a substantial flame sprouting from the end.

"Are you the PI?" the woman with the lighter said.

"John Rockne," I said, holding out my hand.

She took it and said, "Memphis Bornais."

"I think we've met before," I said. "That's an interesting name. A little American South combined with a little, what, French?"

Yeah, I sounded a little stupid, but I never did hold my booze very well.

"Memphis is my songwriter," Shannon said. I nodded, studying her. Memphis had on red velvet pants and a chocolate-brown lace top. The pants were bellbottoms and the sleeves had giant openings. Her age was hard to tell, could have been anywhere from late twenties to early forties. She had shoulder-length brown hair, fine features, and full lips. Kind of like a nicely aged Jennifer Love Hewitt with a little more meat to her.

"Do you write all of Shannon's songs?" I asked her.

"Most," Shannon said. "All the ones I didn't write."

"So what exactly do you do?" Memphis asked and sat down in the chair between Shannon and me. As if on cue, Shannon got up with her empty wine glass.

"I gotta piss," she said by way of explanation. I wondered if the switch had been planned. Was it something I said?

"Investigate," I said to Memphis.

"Investigate what?"

"Whatever someone pays me to do. As long as it isn't illegal or immoral."

"A man with ethics," she said.

"A few. Not all."

She took a hit from a joint.

When she exhaled, she said, "God, the lake is beautiful tonight."

Something about a grown woman sounding like a stoner made me laugh.

"I wish I could see my lighthouse," she said.

"You have a lighthouse?"

"I can see it from my farm on Harsen's," she said, referring to an upscale island a half hour drive from Grosse Pointe. "It's not a bad view, but not as inspiring as this."

"Speaking of inspiration," I said. "Where do you get your ideas for songs? Isn't that what everyone asks?"

She nodded. "How the heck should I know?" she asked. "That's what I want to say."

"What do you usually say?"

"Usually something about pulling things in from life. Or that God just beams them down to me. You know, I tailor the answer depending on the questioner."

"Did you know Jesse Barre?"

She shook her head. "I knew of her guitars, of course. Anyone in the industry knew about them. But no, I didn't know her personally. Why?"

"She makes music. You make music. I figured the two of you would have crossed paths at some point."

"Good guess," she said. "But no. We never did."

"Oh," I said.

We sat in silence for a few moments. A few thoughts ran through my mind.

"How long have you known Shannon?" I said.

"We sort of grew up together," she said. "Went to high school together. Played music together. Fell in and out of touch over the years, but when we both got serious, then we hooked up."

"Did you know Laurence Grasso?"

"Um-hm."

"Did you hear he's dead?"

She nodded.

"Do you care?"

"Not at all."

"Why not?"

"He was a waste of a human being."

"That seems to be the general consensus," I said.

"He treated her like dirt. He was mean. He was cruel. He was stupid but cunning. A weasel," she said. "I'm glad someone sent him on his way."

She was pretty matter-of-fact. I didn't think it was an act.

"Will you turn it into a song?"

"Everything's a song. It's just a matter of writing it down."

Sounded like a tailor-made answer.

I was about to ask another question when I saw her face change. It sort of went slightly pale, and the general din of the crowd went down a notch. I turned and looked over my shoulder.

Shannon's manager stood before me. Teddy Armbruster, his bald head glistening like a Fabergé egg, his tree trunk body immoveable.

"Let's go," he said.

I turned back to Memphis, but she was gone.

I looked back at Teddy, and his dull-blue fish eyes stared back at me.

"Yes, you," he said.

I picked up my glass.

It seemed like the party was over.

Thirty-seven

Teddy lifted the club head until it was an inch from my face.

"Four hundred sixty cc" he said.

I nodded.

"Big Bertha. Titanium. Graphite shaft."

"Very nice," I said.

He leaned down, put a ball on top of a rubber tee and turned his body toward Lake St. Clair. We stood on a little raised platform at the back of the house. It had a patch of Astroturf about nine square yards, and Teddy had his golf bag and clubs leaning against a little wooden rack.

Teddy addressed the ball, and I said, "Keep your head down."

He turned his granite slab of a body and brought the club back in a swift, fluid motion. His body pivoted, and the club bent nearly in half before it sped down with astonishing speed. The ball rocketed off the platform and flew in a direct line out until it made a tiny little splash about three hundred yards away.

"Nice shot," I said. "I think you nailed a muskie. And you didn't even call fore."

"You're funny," he said without even cracking a smile. He lined up another ball and repeated the same effort.

"Got a perch that time," I said. "Do you have someone go out and dive for all those balls?"

"Cheaper just to buy more balls."

"Are golf balls considered pollution?"

In response, he pointed the handle of the club at me and said, "Wanna give it a shot?"

"I've modeled my golf game after Nancy Lopez," I said and took the club. I put a ball on the tee, set down my glass and took a mighty swing. I barely nicked the little pill, and I watched it run off the platform, down to the water's edge until it sat there like a little lake stone.

"Now if we were on the course and that didn't make it past the women's tee," Teddy said, "you'd have to pull your pants down when you walked up to the ball."

"Insult to injury," I noted.

"Why don't you give me that back before you hurt somebody with it," he said.

He took the club and rested it on his boulder of a shoulder. "So what are you doing here, John? Besides disgracing the game of golf?"

"Did you know Larry Grasso?" I said.

"I don't interact with scum," he said. He was bouncing the giant driver off his shoulder. He looked like he was ready to hit me with it. Knock my head into the lake. I'm sure the impression was intended.

"Did you know the scum was killed?"

"I did hear, but I don't care."

Shannon's assistant, Molly, appeared behind me. Had Teddy somehow summoned her?

"Did Shannon still keep in touch with him?"

He laughed. "Are you out of your fucking mind?" He shook his head. "Do me a favor," he said. "Stay away from Shannon. Stay away from me. But even more importantly, stay away from the game of golf, okay?"

He tilted his chin toward Molly. "See Mr. Rockne to the door," he said.

I turned to little Molly and saw that she was now flanked by Erma and Freda.

I glanced back at Teddy. He was in the middle of his backswing. "Thanks for taking the time to bullshit me," I said. His swing caught, and he shanked one about fifty yards to the right. His face turned red.

"Get the fuck out of here," he said.

The Hefty Girls moved up on either side of me, and I lifted my hands up.

"Easy, girls. I'm going. Don't get those gigantic undies of yours in a bundle."

Molly led the way back through the party, and I found myself back at my car.

"Just so you know, I've been told to schedule no more conversations with Shannon for you," Molly said. Her tone was curt and clipped. She extended a hand.

"This will be the last time we talk," she said. Erma and Freda stood behind her, their faces showing all the emotion of rubber caulk.

I shook Molly's hand and felt the soft scrape of paper in my palm.

•

Lakeshore Drive was deserted as always. The lake was choppy, stirred up no doubt by the constant plopping of Teddy Armbruster's Titleist Pro Vs. What an arrogant prick. A guy used to having the world at his feet. A guy living off the natural talent of Shannon Sparrow. A wheeler and a dealer and a fifteen-percent cut of, what, fifteen or twenty million a year? Not bad.

Something told me that Teddy was the kind of guy who could burn a few million bucks a year without batting an eye.

The piece of paper Molly had shoved into my hand now sat on the passenger seat. Subterfuge was surprising coming from the world's most efficiently curt assistant.

I had taken a peek at the note. It was a phone number. Probably a cell. I debated calling it immediately but thought better of it. She'd be at that party for a couple more hours, and I had a feeling that the conversation she wanted to have, that I *hoped* she wanted to have, would be better done in private. Like when she was on her way home from the boss's party.

I looked out at the dark-green water. I'd had too much to drink at the party because I now saw the pale, lifeless eyes of Benjamin Collins. Saw his puffy flesh hanging from his bones in shreds. All because of my colossal mistake.

What a fuckup I was. Usually, I let the feeling pass. Told myself that everyone makes mistakes. Some more egregious than others. But not tonight. Booze sometimes did that to me. Opened up the old wounds and dumped in the salt. How could I have been so stupid? Why didn't I just throw the kid in the back of the squad car and let him sleep it off in his own private cell?

There was no right answer, at least not one I wanted to face.

Thirty-eight

The only thing worse than having a hangover, in my opinion, is being hungover *and* middle-aged. Waking up in a dorm room feeling like shit because of the kegger in Rastelli's room is one thing. Waking up with a hangover and facing your daughters, your mortgage payment, and your middle-aged life is really fucking awful.

"What's wrong?" Anna asked as she shuffled into the kitchen, her bare feet whisking across the wood floor. She had on a pink terrycloth robe, and her hair was piled on top of her head like a standard poodle that's treed a squirrel.

"Too much wine. I hate the fucking French," I said.

"Wine? You don't drink wine."

"Tell that to my liver."

•

An hour later I rolled into my office and enjoyed the peace and quiet for a moment. I'd taken three Tylenol and an extra cup of coffee to help push the headache away. I sat in my chair for a moment and absorbed the silence. I let my conversations with Shannon and Teddy roll around in my mind. Shannon had issues, I was sure of that. Teddy was just an arrogant prick.

I checked my mail and tossed it all, then sat down and fired up the computer. I did a quick Internet search using the name Teddy Armbruster.

All the expected bullshit. Articles about Shannon mostly. The quote from the manager, telling the world what a talented, special, lovely person Shannon was. Extolling her virtues as a songwriter. Her dreams. Her hopes. And of course, her work with charitable causes, namely helping the children.

Blah blah blah.

Of course, with Shannon's name, the search returned only about thirteen thousand items. I closed the search window and picked up the phone.

"Nate," I said. "It's me, John"

"I'm busy," he said.

"So am I."

"Yeah, but the problem is, you're calling me is going to make you less busy and me more busy."

I sighed. "There's a new Chinese place over on Jefferson."

I heard the pause.

"Orchid Gardens?" he said through a mouthful of rapidly rising saliva.

"That's the one."

I pulled the review I'd set aside on my desk from *Metro Times*. Just for this occasion.

"Ginger chicken with a raspberry sauce," I read. "Saffron soup with steamed clams. Rated five out of five stars by the *Metro Times*. Have you been there?"

"I want the buffet," he said.

"The whole thing?"

"The buffet, John."

"Oh mother of mercy," I said.

"Goodbye," he said.

I sighed. With the buffet, the ordeal would turn into a four-hour meal.

"Fine. You got the buffet," I said.

"Okay, what do you want?"

"Teddy Armbruster."

"Never heard of him."

"He's Shannon Sparrow's manager," I said. "I want to know where he's from, what he did pre-Shannon. I think he's evil."

"Oh really."

"Just a hunch."

"An Orchid Garden buffet and we'll know," he said.

"I already said yes."

"I'll call you this afternoon," he said.

"Deal."

We hung up, and I was pleased to note that my headache was gone. Maybe the thought of Chinese food alone was some kind of Eastern cure.

I'd delayed calling the number Molly'd given me because I hoped to learn a little more about Teddy before we talked. But now that it looked like I wouldn't get any dirt for at least a few hours, it was time to make the call.

I punched in the numbers on the slip of paper. Immediately, I heard some gentle static and knew that it was a cell phone.

A voice answered. "Yes?"

"Molly, it's me. John Rockne."

"I'll call you right back," she said, a hint of panic in her voice. The connection was rudely cut. I wondered how she knew where to call me. But then I remembered she could just check her call log.

The phone rang and I picked it up. *That was quick*, I thought.

"John Rockne?" the voice asked.

It wasn't Molly, but I thought I recognized the voice.

"Yes," I said.

"It's Shannon."

"Oh. Hi."

"Is this a bad time?"

"Well, uh, I was expecting another call—"

"I enjoyed talking to you at the party," she said. I heard her take a deep inhale. Cigarette or pot?

"You did?"

"Is that so hard to believe?" she said on her exhale. Probably a joint.

"Well, if you ask me, no, not at all. Talk to my friends though . . ."

"I just wondered if we could meet somewhere and talk," she said. "Do you have somewhere private we could get together?"

"Like, how private?" I said. Boy, this was weird. Shannon Sparrow wanting to meet me somewhere privately? After she says she enjoyed conversing with me?

"What do you think?" she said.

"How about my office?"

Her silence told me that wasn't what she had in mind.

Oh boy. I ran through a few options, one of which included saying no. I dismissed it though.

"I have a sailboat at Windmill Pointe," I said. It was a piece of shit fixer-upper that I'd been meaning to work on for years. Anna and I just kept it to keep the boat slip. There's about a ten-year waiting period for those slips.

"Private marina?" she said.

"Even better," I said, "It's public and totally empty this time of year. No guard to see your car, no attendants to recognize you. Just park in the parking lot and walk to my slip. No one will know you're there."

"Perfect," she said.

I gave Shannon directions then said, "I'm in slip forty-eight. *Air Fare* is the name of the boat."

"*Air Fare*?"

"I bought it from a pilot," I said. "I know, stupid name."

"I can be there tonight."

"So around ten?" I said.

"Okay."

We hung up without saying goodbye. Before I could even contemplate just how weird this was getting, the phone rang again.

"It's me."

I recognized the voice as Molly's. Were she and Shannon trading phones? Handing it back and forth, laughing at how easy it was to trick me?

"I wanted to warn you," she said. It sounded like she was walking somewhere, probably outside.

"Warn me about what?"

"You've asked a lot of questions, and there are people who don't want you to get the answers," she said.

"Like who?"

"Look, don't make this difficult—"

"Too late," I said. "People have died. It's already difficult."

"Don't make it *more* difficult then. Enough people have been hurt."

I had a hunch and played it. "Is that the real reason you called? Just to warn me? Or do you know something I could use? Something that could help?"

She paused just a second, and I knew I was right. "I know it's all about Jesse Barre," she said.

"Yeah, but—"

I heard another voice, in the background. It sounded like a man's, and I thought I heard him say Molly's name. Immediately, her voice took on a different tone.

"Look, just make sure the invoices are sent with the proper postage," Molly barked at me. I waited, wondering who had interrupted her. "Okay, okay," she said, this time the panic in her voice was clear. "Right, I'll put it in the mail to you, okay? I'll send it to your office. Right?"

"Send it via a courier today," I said, understanding.

"Fine. Just don't let this mistake happen again!" she said and then hung up.

Message received, I thought. Did Shannon Sparrow get a lot of invoices? I wondered. Well, creativity wouldn't be at the top of my list for attributes Molly would have. She seemed like a law-and-order, by-the-book kind of gal. But the important thing was that she said she'd send whatever it was to my office. I felt like a linebacker who'd broken through the line and was in the backfield, ready to knock the quarterback on his ass.

Okay, I thought. *Shannon at ten o'clock tonight.*

Nate would call me this afternoon.

That left me a few hours.

Just enough time to chat with my client.

Thirty-nine

I found him gardening. A grown man, on his knees in the backyard with dirt all over his arms and his face streaked with peat moss. Some guys go to Florida and play bocce. Clarence digs in the ground. To each his own.

"Aren't you supposed to plant 'em deeper than that?" I asked. The little shrubs slash bushes he was planting . . . you could see the ball of roots sticking out a little bit.

Clarence shook his head. "They'll drown if you plant them any deeper."

I nodded.

He took off his gloves and tossed them into a little plastic cart he had next to him. It held a few more of the bushes as well as a variety of clippers and shears and digging tools.

"Speaking of drowning," Clarence said. "Why don't you go into the kitchen, find a couple of cold beers, and meet me over there." He gestured to a little bench that sat in the shade of a big maple tree. I followed his instructions to a tee and rejoined my gray-bearded friend with two companions from the Anheuser-Busch brewery in St. Louis.

As Clarence sipped his beer, I brought him up to speed on everything that had happened.

"So you think Shannon Sparrow's ex-husband killed Jesse?" he said.

I nodded. "I can't prove it yet, but yeah, I think he did."

"Why?"

"That's the big question really," I said. "I can't answer it right now. I've got a couple of hunches that I'm working on."

"It doesn't make any sense to me," Clarence said. "You're convinced Nevada Hornsby had nothing to do with it?"

"He didn't kill her," I said. "He loved her."

"Lots of men kill women they really love. Happens all the time."

"I don't deny that," I said. "I just don't believe it was the case here."

He took another long drink, and his bottle was empty. He tossed it twenty feet through the air where it landed in his little gardening cart.

"Nice shot," I said.

It had been easier for him to cope by targeting his anger toward someone. But now he had to face the fact that he may have been wrong.

"You can help me," I said.

"Tell me what you need."

"I need to learn more about how star musicians work. Shannon Sparrow has such a fucking huge entourage. Managers, assistants, writers, hangers-on. I feel lost. Who has daily contact with Shannon? Who might be so involved with Shannon that they would resort to murder?"

"Forget the assistants," Clarence said. "I wasn't much of a star, but I had a bit of an entourage."

"That's why I thought I'd ask you."

"My assistants came and went," he said. "Never could remember their names. Usually the manager doesn't get too involved on a day-to-day basis. Manages from a big office in New York or L.A. Makes a phone call to the record label, charges the star twenty grand."

"Good work if you can get it."

"The band mates . . . it all depends on the star. Some are close to their players. Some fire them without batting an eye."

"Hired hands," I said.

He nodded. "A producer will say, 'Here are the tracks, learn them in six weeks or we'll find someone who can.' Of course, that's not always true. Some guys in the band are key in developing songs and so on, then they're very valuable and have a lot at stake."

"What about songwriters?"

Clarence shrugged. "They can be very valuable. But as far as a daily involvement . . . I don't think so. Usually they're perched in some house in Malibu, looking at the Pacific, banging out hooks."

I thought about it. "A lot of what you just told me doesn't seem to fit Shannon Sparrow," I said. "Her manager seems very involved. Her band mates all hang out. Her assistant. They seem to all be there all the time."

"Like I said, I was a very minor player. And that was a long time ago," Clarence said. "Times have changed. I don't have a lot of ideas on what a Shannon Sparrow situation might be."

"Okay."

"I can tell you one thing that I'm sure hasn't changed."

"Shoot."

"They're all there for the money," he said. "And in Shannon's case, it's big money. More money than we can probably imagine. So despite all the relationships, the hanging out, it's all crap. It was that way with me back when I played. Everybody acted like friends but it was always all about the money."

"The music is incidental."

"In most cases, yeah. Sometimes the songwriter is the only one genuinely into the creation of music. But I've met plenty of jaded songwriters too. They think what they sell is crap. The signer thinks it's crap. The manager thinks it's crap. But they all fucking love it when the royalty checks come in."

"Do you think that's how Shannon is?"

He shrugged. "My guess would be yes, that's how she is. But everyone's different. When she was a struggling young girl with a guitar, maybe those early songs came right from her heart. Maybe they poured out of her soul. And then the businessmen rushed in and mined her like a sliver of gold in rock. And then maybe it all changed. Who knows?"

I nodded and polished off my beer. I stood up.

"If Hornsby didn't kill her," he started to say then stopped. I watched his face contort with anger and grief. I didn't know where he was going with this. It turned out, he wasn't going anywhere. He stopped. So I finished the thought for him.

"I'll find out who did."

•

It turned out that Nate couldn't wait for his payment, so we met at the Orchid Gardens for the buffet. The maitre d' gave Nate a look that was probably the same expression Custer wore when he realized he wasn't just going to lose, but he was going to lose big.

Nate didn't disappoint. He loaded a plate full of all the fried stuff first: egg rolls, crab wontons, chicken.

"Lubes up the pipes," he explained to me.

I got a big plate of chicken fried rice with an egg roll, tossed on some soy sauce, and sat across from him. Watching Nate eat Chinese buffet was like watching a conveyor belt dump ingots into a blast furnace.

"Your boy is bad news," he finally said, after most of his first plate was demolished. Nate signaled the waitress over and ordered a beer, went up to the buffet, and loaded on mostly chicken things: garlic chicken, sweet-and-sour chicken, Kung Pao chicken.

I stuck with my water and rice.

"Or at least, he *was* bad news," Nate continued, pausing every now and then to clean the various sauces and juices that accumulated in the corners of his mouth.

Once Nate had demolished his second plate, I figured he'd take a moment to tell me what he'd found. I was right. He pushed away plate number two and pulled out a notebook.

"Teddy Armbruster, as you know him, was born in Chicago as Edward Abrucci," he said. "Born in Chicago in 1960. First arrested at age twelve. Assault. More arrests through his teens, which earned him a stay at the juvenile correctional facility near Rockford, Illinois."

Nate flipped to the next page of his notebook. "Apparently our man moved to Detroit after he was released. His crime pattern changed too. He graduated from assaults and robberies to extortion."

"Mob?"

Nate nodded. "As his crimes became more 'organized,' to make a bad pun, his arrests disappeared. His last brush with the law was in 1987 for extortion. He beat it. Since then, he's been clean."

I thought about that while Nate went back up to the buffet. Now he was moving on to seafood: more crab wontons, lobster with soybeans, and shrimp fried rice.

"So do you think he's really clean now? Has he gone legit?" I asked Nate when he got back to the table.

He shrugged his shoulders and shoveled in the food. "He could be clean or just a whole lot more polished," he said.

"So far three people have been murdered," I said. "Jesse Barre. Larry Grasso. And Rufus Coltraine. All people within his orbit."

"They were in a lot of other people's orbits too," Nate said, soy sauce dripping down his chin.

"Maybe Shannon had killed Jesse for her guitars, then framed her husband for it," I suggested.

"And why would a woman worth about a hundred million dollars need to kill someone for guitars? They were expensive, but not that expensive."

"Had to be the ex-husband then," I said. "He was still in love with Shannon, tried to win her back by killing Jesse Barre and stealing her guitars. And then he framed Coltrane for it. They were buddies in prison."

Nate stopped eating. I knew it was big if he stopped eating.

"They were?"

I nodded. "I talked to a guy I know at Jackson."

"So you think that was the case?" he said.

"It's a definite possibility. But I don't think Grasso was working alone. Someone was pulling his strings, maybe using his love for Shannon against him."

"Maybe it was Shannon herself."

I shook my head. "I don't think so. I heard the woman speak. It wasn't Shannon. I didn't recognize the voice."

Nate pushed his plate away from him and belched, a low rumbling passage of gas that reminded me of a coal mine being exhumed.

"Don't mess with this guy, John," he finally said. "I think people who fuck with Teddy Armbruster end up being hurt. And hurt badly."

"Someone else may be fucking with Teddy Armbruster. And it isn't me."

•

By the time I got back to my office, it was late. The only people more tired than me were the guys at the Chinese restaurant in charge of replenishing the buffet.

I checked my watch. Nearly five o'clock. I checked the mail for a package from Molly but no dice. Most courier services finished up by six. I had a bad feeling in my gut, and it was only partially from watching Nate ingest the caloric equivalent of a small family.

Whatever Molly had intended to send me should have been here by now. I wondered about the interruption. Had the man heard Molly? Was she in trouble?

I weighed the pros and cons of waiting. It didn't take long. Sitting around waiting for a courier made little sense. I thought about calling, but that didn't seem like a good idea either. She was constantly in someone's presence. Someone who was always listening. It would be better just to show up. Be the asshole PI who needed to be dealt with. That chore would fall to the lowly personal assistant.

Besides, with a sinking feeling in the pit of my guts, I wondered, *what if the courier never comes?*

The drive back to Shannon Sparrow's temporary compound took less than five minutes, but as I pulled closer, I saw that someone had gotten there ahead of me.

Blue and red flashing lights pulled me closer. *Please, God, no,* I thought. *Don't let this happen.*

The driveway was choked with police cars. I pulled over into the grass next to the driveway and jogged toward the door. A cop stopped me, a thick-necked bull with a shiny black crew cut. I didn't recognize him, and I didn't see Ellen around.

I looked past him and saw Erma and Freda being questioned by two detectives.

And on the floor was a body.

Even from here I could see that it was a small body. Swimming in a large pool of blood.

Molly.

Forty

"How did you manage to get here before me?" a voice asked. I turned, and Ellen walked toward me, her thumbs hooked in her gun belt.

I was staring out at Lake St. Clair. The water was smooth and green, waiting for a giant freighter to plow through the center of its body.

I couldn't stop thinking about how another life had been taken and how Molly had tried to get in touch with me. I should have done more. I should have driven to see her immediately after her call was interrupted. *Goddamnit*, I thought.

"John," my sister said.

"I should have known," I said.

"Just start at the beginning," she said. So I did. I detailed my conversation with Molly, the note with the phone number, waiting for a courier that never showed up, and the decision to drive over here on my own.

Ellen didn't respond when I finished.

"So what's your best guess?" she said.

"Honestly," I said. "I have no clue."

"You don't know what she was trying to get to you?"

I shook my head. Ellen turned and looked out at the lake.

"Her neck was broken," she said. "Apparently."

"Ah, Jesus."

217

"They're saying she fell down the stairs."

That brought me off the car. "You've gotta be fucking kidding me. Fell down the stairs? I don't think so."

"No other signs of injury. Two witnesses say they saw it happen."

"The pork queens? Erma and Freda?"

"They heard a loud crash," Ellen said. "Rushed in and found the victim at the foot of the steps." I could tell Ellen wasn't buying it either; she was just laying out the official story so far.

"Oh my God," I said. "What total bullshit."

"It isn't bullshit until it's *proven* to be bullshit." I heard what she was saying.

"If it's the last goddamned thing I do," I said.

I kept thinking of Molly. Of her crisp way of speaking, her little daily planner clutched to her chest. So in control. And then the vision of her sprawled out at the base of the stairs.

"We did a quick search on the vic," Ellen said. "She looks clean as a whistle. No record, not even a speeding ticket."

I thought about my interaction with Molly. Precise. Efficient. Maybe a tad on the cold side. But that was her job. To protect her boss.

It looked now like she should have been a little more worried about protecting herself. Whatever it was she'd found, she was trying to get to me. But why me? If it had something to do with the murder of Jesse Barre, why not go to the cops? I knew the answer as soon as I asked the question.

She was worried about what might happen to her.

So she was going to let me get the evidence.

In short, she wanted me to take the fall.

I winced at the irony.

•

Ellen went back into the crime scene where I still wasn't allowed, so I turned my attention once again to the lake. When you lived in Grosse Pointe, you couldn't help but associate the lake with events in your life. Lake St. Clair sat there, a silent witness of the community next to it. I had my own personal history with the lake. Culminating in the death of Benjamin Collins. His life ended in the lake. Along with what used to be mine.

And now, here I was back at the lake, working a case that was spiraling out of control. Every one of my instincts told me that my meeting with Shannon later tonight was a setup. Shannon luring me to the park after dark. The death of her assistant only a few hours old. Someone was trying to tie up loose ends.

But I didn't believe Shannon was in on it. She was kooky. She played the star thing to the hilt. But for some reason, I didn't think she was a killer. Maybe I'd been taken in a bit by her beauty. No, not her beauty. The warmth of her beauty. Some women are beautiful like crystal. Cold, cool lines. Others have the beauty of a glowing fire. I felt Shannon was the latter.

But I'd been wrong plenty of times before.

Something was nagging at me. Like a hair-trigger on the verge of being pulled. My mind kept going back to Laurence Grasso. He was a trigger too.

Rufus Coltraine had been the second to die. There was something about his role in this thing too. Something about him that kept coming back to my mind but I just couldn't put my finger on it. Something about—

Family.

And then something sparked in my mind. Family. Joe Puhy, the prison guard at Jackson had said he thought Coltraine would head South to see his family. So why hadn't he? And Puhy had said that Coltraine didn't get any letters—so how did he know he had family in . . . where was it?

219

Goddamnit. I pulled out my cell phone. I almost had it, and then it would slip away. If Puhy worked at Jackson, he probably lived in the area. There were only a few small towns nearby. Plymouth. Ann Arbor.

I punched in the number for information and asked for Joe Puhy's number. There were three of them. I jotted them down and called the first. I got a machine, but when the voice of the answering machine clicked on, I knew I didn't have the right one. The Puhy I'd spoken to was older and gruff.

Exactly the voice I got on the second try.

"I'm very sorry to bother you at home, Mr. Puhy," I said. "This is John Rockne, the private investigator. We spoke earlier about Rufus Coltraine and Laurence Grasso."

"Oh yeah," he said, not happy at all. "I remember. Look, we're about to sit down to dinner." I could hear voices in the background.

"I'm terribly sorry, sir. This won't take more than a minute."

He sighed. "You're a friend of House, right?"

House was my buddy who worked on Cell Block A, who'd initially put me in touch with Puhy. Thank God for House. I owed him one.

"Yeah," I said.

"All right, go ahead."

"I was just looking back through my notes, and I saw that you said you thought Rufus Coltraine would go down South to see his family. Or that you thought he had family there."

"Uh-huh." More dishes clattering in the background. I had to make this fast.

"But you also said that you didn't recall him getting any letters or anything from family members," I said.

There was a pause as Puhy thought about the contradiction.

"Uh . . . right."

"So how did you know he had family down there?"

This time the pause was longer. I heard more voices in the background, including a woman calling out, "Joe!" She had that kind of voice that you ignored at your own peril. Kind of like my wife's.

"Uh . . ." he said.

Shit, I didn't want to lose him.

"You know, this is really a bad time," Puhy said.

"I know it is, but another person has died, Mr. Puhy." I was starting to get mad. People were dying, and this guy's Beef Fucking Stroganoff was more important.

He must have heard the tone in my voice.

"Hold on!" he shouted to the people in the background.

"All right," he said. "Let me think." We both waited. A freighter nosed its way out of the Detroit River, heading north. The clatter of silverware sounded from the Puhy kitchen.

"Okay, I think I remember," he said.

"Shoot."

"It wasn't a letter or anything," he said. "I think I overheard him talking about it."

"Was he talking about it with Laurence Grasso?"

"Yeah. How'd you know that?"

"Just a hunch."

"Yeah, I think I overheard Coltraine saying something about getting out and going there."

"Where, Mr. Puhy?"

"Home," he said.

"Home where?"

"I'm pretty sure it was, um, Tennessee."

A shiver ran down my spine. The little thing that had been dancing around in my brain finally let itself be known.

"Where in Tennessee?" I asked, even though I already knew.

A giant block had slammed into place.

"Memphis," he said.

Forty-one

Something about a house. Fuck. I was losing my mind: short-term, medium-term and long-term memory loss. All at the same time. I pounded the steering wheel with my hands. *Think, think, think*. I pulled onto Vernier from Lakeshore, heading toward I-94.

I needed to start making more connections. That feeling of being close wasn't good enough.

Where had I been when I felt things starting to come together? At the party. The first time. Talking to Shannon's entourage for the first time.

A car pulled in front of me, and I reefed the wheel to the right, sped up, and floored it past him.

Something about a farmhouse?

What the fuck was it? We were all sitting around, talking about escapes or something. And Memphis mentioned something about looking at a house. Was she buying?

Finally, it clicked.

A lighthouse. That's right, a lighthouse. Because she said she was on Harsen's. The island at the other end of Lake St. Clair.

I pounded the wheel again and roared onto I-94. Harsen's Island. A lighthouse. And someone had said something about Memphis milking cows. A joke that I assumed meant she had a little farm or something. Farms on Harsen's weren't unheard of.

I glanced at the clock on the dashboard.

It'd been nearly three hours since Molly had been killed. If the same person was headed for Memphis', he or she had a big jump on me.

I pushed the pedal all the way to the floor.

•

Harsen's Island is the biggest of a small group of islands at the north end of Lake St. Clair. The lake narrows and eventually turns into the St. Clair River for a brief thirty miles or so before opening back up, this time into Lake Huron.

I exited I-94, sped across Harper and pulled into the parking lot at the ferry harbor. Fifteen minutes later, the ferry dumped us on the island, and I hit the road running. Even though Harsen's has its own yacht club and for years was a miniature summer playground for Grosse Pointers, it still feels like you travel back twenty years or so. Mostly summer cottages and the occasional bait shop/convenience store.

The entire island is only a couple square miles with one main road that runs along the outside border. The road is aptly named Harsen's Boulevard, and I steered onto it from the ferry dock. It had been over fifteen years since I'd been on the island, and then I was a high-schooler driving out to my buddy's cottage to get drunk.

I'd never seen a lighthouse on the island, or if I had, I certainly didn't remember, didn't know that one even existed out here.

I also figured there weren't many cops out here either. So I hammered the pedal down and turned Harsen's into my own private Indianapolis 500.

After about five minutes, I sped around a steep curve and saw the lighthouse—although, technically, it was more like a light post you see in the suburbs. A tiny harbor had a few boats tied off, and I looked at the surrounding land.

No sign of a farmhouse.

I did, however, see an older woman walking a Bassett Hound. I pulled the car up next to her.

"Do you know of a farmhouse around here with a view of the lighthouse? It belongs to a songwriter named Memphis Bornais?" I said.

She looked at me with bloodshot blue eyes. They looked just like the dogs'. I thought she was going to tell me that Harsen's residents were a private people and that if this Memphis woman wanted me to find her she would've given me directions.

Instead, she jerked an unusually large thumb in the direction behind her.

"Third mailbox down," she said. The Bassett Hound gave a soft bark, and they went on their way.

I thanked her and sped down to the mailbox—instead of the little flag sticking up from the box it was a metal musical note. I knew I had the right place.

The driveway was dirt and gravel, and it immediately climbed. From the road, the tall trees blocked any view of the houses behind. But once I got near the top of the driveway, I realized there was a very small bluff. And perched on top was a little white farmhouse, with a picket fence and a red barn behind it.

It was a cross between Mayberry and Martha's Vineyard, before Billy Joel moved in.

I skidded to a stop in the roughly hewn semi-circular drive and jogged to the front door. I rang the doorbell and waited, but I heard nothing from inside. I tried the knob. Locked.

I ran to the back of the house and saw a silver 7 Series BMW backed up against the house. I went up the back porch steps and was about to knock on the door when I saw that it was already open.

I went through it, into a small mudroom. There were potted plants and gardening gloves and an umbrella. The door leading from the mudroom into the kitchen was open as well. Inside the kitchen, I saw a few dishes in the sink, a pot on the stove, and a small cat bowl with food in it.

From the kitchen, I went through a doorway into a small dining room and off the dining room was a living room. The place was furnished with big, overstuffed chairs and throw rugs. A small fireplace sat off to one side of the living room. I saw on the mantle a collection of photographs.

To my right, I saw a stairwell and heard a bumping noise from above me.

"Hello!" I yelled up. No one answered.

I climbed the stairs two at a time and came to a hallway with three doors. The first door on my right was open, and I could see tile as well as the edge of a pedestal sink.

To my left was another door, closed. And straight ahead, the third door was open, and I could see shadows moving inside. I walked forward, my heart beating from exertion and fear.

For the first time in my career, I desperately wished for a gun.

I peeked into the room and immediately understood the bumping sound and the moving shadows.

Memphis hung from the ceiling fan, her neck stretched in a way that could mean only one thing. The ceiling fan was on, slowly spinning her body, her foot occasionally bumping against the bed's footboard.

I froze, unable to tear myself away from the image of Memphis' face, her lips frozen in a look of terror, blood dripping from her nose—

Blood dripping . . .

Fresh blood . . .

An electric spike shot down my spine just as I heard the whisper of a shoe on carpet, and I ducked, but the blow cracked along my vertebrae between my shoulder blades. I hit the floor. I rolled and caught the sight of

Erma's—or was it Freda's?—face flushed red, her teeth gritted, a Taser in her hand.

She cursed in German, and I rolled into the bedroom where Memphis hung.

And I rolled right under Freda.

She'd been standing behind the door. While her sister had been in the bedroom with the door closed. As I watched them descend on me, I realized they knew I was coming. Somehow, they knew. They'd staged the scene to lure me in.

The first one pounced on me, sat on my chest, and pinned my arms under her knees. I tried to head-butt her in the face, but she pulled back easily, and all I caught was air. I felt an incredible weight on my legs and realized the other one was kneeling on them.

If I had any doubts about what they were trying to do, those doubts ended when the first one grabbed a handful of my hair and brought her gun up toward my mouth. I gritted my teeth, but she let go of my hair, brought her forearm down and pinched my nose shut.

I held my breath, knowing what was going to happen. When I opened my mouth to breathe, she would jam the gun in and blow off the top of my head.

Then they would jot a little note.

Double suicide. Or murder/suicide depending on which story they went with.

I'd killed Memphis for some reason, and then they'd bring out my past. An ex-cop ate his gun. Happens all the fucking time. Every day, in fact.

I didn't think my sister would let it ride, but hey, these two fuckers were pros. They'd make it look very good, very real.

My lungs were on fire, and I knew I couldn't hold my breath very much longer. The first one had a little smile on her face. She looked like a mean little kid who'd pulled the wings off a fly and was now happily watching it die a pathetic little spasmodic death.

It pissed me off.

Every muscle in my body slammed into place, and I bucked with everything I had.

The first one barely moved.

But move she did.

Just enough to free my left arm.

I reached up and got her neck and bucked again, this time bringing her head toward me as I rammed my head forward. I heard and felt her nose squash against my forehead. Blood sprayed, and now my right arm was loose. I grabbed the gun as the woman on top of me sagged. The gun fired a round, and the explosion brought the three of us into a burst of frantic energy.

I'd hoped that I'd knocked the first one out, but her eyes cleared just as I was bringing the gun around. She had the advantage, but I had momentum on my side. I gave one more shove, and the gun came around toward her chest.

I pulled the trigger.

Just as she was knocked back, the second one let go of my legs and reached for her gun. I put three rounds into her chest, and she staggered back into the hallway and fell on her ass, her feet still in the room. She had a look of utter sadness, looking down at her dead sister. She toppled over then, her big body landing with a thud.

The smell of gunpowder was overwhelming, and I felt stars shooting across my forehead.

Everything started to go black, and I was suddenly scared I'd been shot.

But then I realized why.

I was still holding my breath.

Forty-two

The first thing I did was vomit. I made it to the toilet, worrying about destroying evidence, but hurl I did. My whole body was shaking, probably from both fear and the aftermath of having an ungodly amount of volts shot through my system. I was having a near-death *and* an out-of-body experience at the same time.

Somehow, I found my way back to the first bedroom, where one of the twins had been hiding. I assumed the note was meant to be written in my hand, and sure enough, there was a slip of paper. It was the one on which I'd jotted down my name and phone number and given to someone in Shannon's entourage, maybe Molly?

It was standard, depressed prose: *"God forgive me, I'm a failure . . ."* The note said I had begun an affair with Memphis, fallen in love, and when I told her it was over because I was a relatively happily married man, she killed herself. Which then weighed so heavily on me that I could only deal with it by killing myself as well.

The note stopped there, probably when I entered the house and interrupted the forger at work.

I thought about what to do next. I should call the police. *Yes, call the police.* They would arrive, I'd make my statement, a few hours of questioning, and I'd be released around midnight. *No, don't call the police.* I stood there, shaking, trying to pull myself together.

Shit. I checked my watch. It was late—I would have to hurry to make my meeting with Shannon.

Leaving the scene of a crime was a felony. So was killing people, and I had two dead bodies to my name, and a third hanging from a ceiling fan.

With the old woman and the hound, and the people on the ferry, I knew there was no way I could avoid facing the cops. The question was: when *did* I want to face them? Leaving the scene of a crime would be more than enough to have my PI license revoked.

Still, I was hot on this thing, and I had a feeling that my meeting with Shannon would bring it to an end.

I decided to compromise. First, I did a quick run-through of Memphis' house, looking for anything that I could use with Shannon. It felt good to be moving, to be doing something.

I went through every room in the house but came up empty. There was no other choice. I left the house and made a beeline for the silver BMW. It was either Memphis' or the twins', but I didn't know which.

I looked inside and saw a bag in the front passenger seat's floor space. It struck a chord with me, and for some reason, I didn't think it belonged to one of the twins.

In fact, I could've sworn that I'd seen the bag somewhere. It looked neat and organized, made of brown leather. I could see the Franklin planner inside.

I had seen the bag before.

It was Molly's.

I tried the door and found it was locked. At the back of the house was a small flower bed with a border of river rocks. I picked up the biggest rock, went back, and smashed in the Beemer's window.

The alarm went off, and I grabbed the bag.

On the way back to my car, I lived up to the other end of my compromise.

I called my sister.

She didn't like what I had to say.

Forty-three

I wasn't really in the best shape. I ached from the Taser blast and a blow one of the twins had laid on my spine. But mostly I was in shock from killing two women. The sight of blood, especially my own, made me very uncomfortable. And right now, I was doing everything I could to not think about what had taken place at Memphis' farmhouse. I'm sure the cops were there by now, wondering where I was, scouring the scene, trying to figure out what had happened.

I couldn't bring myself to tell Ellen where I was going. Suffice it to say, if there was any way to reach through the phone line and strangle someone, she would have popped my head off like a champagne cork.

Now I was just trying to keep it together.

I was early for my rendezvous with Shannon. I parked my car in the Windmill Pointe Marina parking lot and hurried out to the dock. The wind was picking up, and the chop had graduated from stiff to severe. Above me, the night sky showed no stars, and I could see the black inkiness of serious storm clouds.

The benches normally taken by fishermen going after the perch that hung out close to shore were empty. As were the picnic tables and beach chairs. The whole fucking place was empty except for me.

And maybe Shannon Sparrow.

•

A flash of lightning threw a spotlight on the lake. There wasn't a single boat. Even the buoys looked like they wanted to come in and get out of the wind.

My boat was called *Air Fare* because it was owned by some pilot who'd had money to burn, but then lost his job. I had a feeling it was due to drinking, because when I took ownership of the boat and went down below, the smell of gin was overwhelming. Something told me that the pilot was most likely never far from a martini. A man after my own heart, to be honest. I could use about a baker's dozen of martinis right now.

It had occurred to me that maybe someone had dropped Shannon off. After all, a woman of her stature usually had a driver. Maybe she'd had someone drop her off then would call to have someone pick her up. I hadn't noticed anyone in the parking lot. There weren't even any cars, other than a black pickup truck and a white Toyota Tercel, both of which I knew belonged to park workers.

The boat looked just like I'd left it. The dark-red spinnaker cover was snapped into place. The mooring lines were all taut. The deck was neat and clean.

There was no sign of Shannon.

I turned back toward the parking lot. No sense standing out there waiting for her. I boarded the boat and unlocked the doors to the cabin down below.

The smell was a mixture of marine oil, gasoline, booze, and cleaning products.

I flipped on the generator and turned on some of the interior lights, careful to make sure the curtains were drawn. A glimpse into Molly's briefcase had confirmed the rising feeling. Things were falling into place, and this meeting with Shannon was going to prove everything I believed to be right.

At least, that's what I hoped.

•

"John?"

I heard her voice from the pier. I'd been lost in thought but now stepped up onto the deck and called back. "Shannon."

She had on blue jeans, a windbreaker, and topsiders. A large bag was slung over her shoulder. Her hair was loosely pulled back. She looked . . . normal.

"Nice boat," she said.

"It's a tub of shit, but thanks," I said.

She stood there, uncertain. It was odd seeing her by herself. No gang of hangers-on swarming around like a pack of bloodthirsty mosquitoes. She seemed smaller, less sure of herself. Maybe I was reading too much into it.

She stepped off the main dock and walked along the dividing dock between my boat and the one next to me.

I held her hand as she hopped onto the deck. Without saying a word, she went down the stairs to the cabin. After taking a quick look around and seeing nothing out of the ordinary, I followed her below.

The cabin's layout was simple. On one side was a small table surrounded by a U-shaped bench. The other side was a long counter with a sink, a fridge, and a radio. Small storage compartments were tucked everywhere in between.

I gestured for Shannon to sit on one end of the bench, and I took the other. The space was too small to sit face to face, so she sat straight ahead and I sat with my legs out toward the stairs.

"Okay, who called this meeting?" I said.

"What happened to your face?" she asked.

"You'll find out soon enough," I said.

"What's that supposed to mean?"

"How come you haven't said a word about Molly's death?" I said, ignoring her question. I mean, come on, your assistant falls down the stairs, breaks her neck, and you keep an appointment to meet a PI at ten o'clock at night? It was about as absurd as me killing two people and keeping an appointment with a country music star. Chaos reigned.

"I guess I'm all talked out about it," she said. "I've been over it with the cops nine or ten times."

"Now that you've got your story straight, why don't you lay it on me?"

"I had nothing to do with it," she said. "And don't talk to me like that."

"You weren't there when she died?"

She shook her head. "Do you have anything to drink around here?" she said. "Aren't sailors always supposed to have booze on hand?"

I hesitated and took a look at the big purse she'd slid off her shoulder and placed on the table.

"Oh please," she said.

It was a moment of truth of sorts. Did I think Shannon was knee-deep in this thing? The bigger question was: how could she not be? But as I looked at her across the table, my gut told me she wasn't. I got up, went to the sideboard, and grabbed a bottle of whiskey, splashing some into a clean glass for her.

"You're not drinking?" she said.

"You need me to?" I said.

She shrugged her shoulders.

I waited while Shannon drained half the glass in one big gulp. The boat rocked slightly, and I knew that the wind had picked up even more, if it was able to whip waves that big into the harbor.

"I don't know what's going on," she said.

With a shaking hand, she reached for her purse. I watched her as she pulled out a thick joint and a lighter. As

233

she tried to light the tip, it slipped from her hand and landed on the floor.

"Just tell me what you do know," I said.

"I can't," she said, her voice quavering. "I have people who are supposed to do that for me."

"That's the problem, isn't it?" I said.

She nodded.

"Too many people doing too many things on your behalf," I said. It didn't seem to register for a moment. When it did, she went pale, and it was hard to see her as the superstar in the press. On the covers of magazines and the object of countless fan clubs and websites. She looked like a scared, lonely woman approaching middle-age.

"Please help me," she said. "Tell me what's going on." Her lips trembled, and the tears started rolling down her cheeks. "Do you know what's going on?" she asked.

I let out a long breath. "I think I do."

"Can you explain it to me?"

I took the CD from Molly's purse, the one I'd found in the twins' silver BMW. I went to the control panel of the boat where a small, built-in CD player was housed. I flicked on the power button and slid the disc in. I waited a moment and then hit play.

It was just static at first. Almost like a gentle scratching. And then soft, acoustic guitar. Gentle notes, full of sorrow and melancholy.

And then a voice.

A really beautiful, haunting voice that sang of lost love and the ghosts of lovers past.

I was listening at last to Jesse Barre.

The music itself was rough, but you could hear the quality, the command of the song and the ease of the voice. She sounded like a natural. But it was the power of the words that moved me the most. It was the kind of song that if you heard it on the radio, you would wait and hope the DJ would tell you who it was, so you could immediately go buy the CD.

I looked at Shannon, and I could tell she knew the same thing. The fear in her face was gone, replaced with a kind of warm recognition. Even in the midst of murder and mayhem, she was enough of a human being and a musician to recognize true beauty when she heard it. And she was hearing it now.

When the song was over, I turned back to the player and hit pause.

I heard clapping and when I turned back, Teddy Armbruster stood next to Shannon.

And next to Teddy was a man.

He looked oddly familiar to me. He had a smirk on his lean, slightly wolfish face.

The boat seemed to sway under me, and my knees felt weak. I reached out with my hand against the side of the cabinet to steady myself.

"Surprise, surprise," Teddy said.

The man just looked at me, curious amusement on his face.

It was him.

The man who I'd met on a snowy night so many years ago.

"Look at him . . . he's in shock," Teddy said.

I couldn't stop looking at the man. I opened my mouth to speak but nothing came out.

Teddy spoke again, a wide smile on his face.

"I'd introduce you," Teddy said, unable to suppress a chuckle. "But I believe you two have already met."

It was him.

The man who'd killed Benjamin Collins.

Forty-four

"Why don't you step away from the CD player, John?" Teddy said. On cue, the man who'd killed Benjamin Collins eased out a handgun from a shoulder holster.

"Take out the CD and hand it to me," Teddy said.

I did as asked.

"Teddy, what are you doing?" Shannon said.

Teddy smiled at her, took the CD, and slipped it into the breast pocket of his suit coat.

"Nothing you need to worry about, Shannon."

"But I do," she said. She turned to me. "That was Jesse Barre singing, wasn't it?"

I nodded. "And singing beautifully," I added, still not taking my eyes from the man across from me.

"What a shame," Teddy said.

"John," Shannon said. She was looking at the final destination, but wasn't sure how we'd gotten here.

"Jesse Barre was going to retire from making guitars," I said. "Her boyfriend, Nevada Hornsby, told me she was taking a sabbatical."

"Permanent sabbatical," Teddy said. "An oxymoron, I suppose." His smirk was vile.

"At the time, I didn't know what it meant," I said. I was about to ramble, but I didn't know what else to do. No one was stopping me, and I needed some time to try to figure something out.

"But then when I found the CD in Molly's purse—the one Erma and Freda had killed her for—I started to realize what happened," I said. "Jesse had contacted Memphis, probably for advice. Memphis lied to me about not knowing Jesse. Memphis was probably threatened by it, worried that Shannon would start buying Jesse's songs, so she convinced Laurence Grasso that when he got out of prison, if he killed Jesse for her, Memphis would try to get him back with Shannon."

"Oh my God," Shannon said.

"Oh please," Teddy said. He was bored, looking around the inside of my sailboat with obvious disgust. The man with the gun was only looking at me.

"And Grasso set Coltraine up to take the fall."

"This isn't true," Shannon said.

"I think at some point, when Grasso was out of control, Memphis went to Teddy and spilled the beans," I said. "Somehow, Molly realized what was going on and, ever the spin doctor, Teddy had both Memphis and Molly killed. And now he'll try to kill me. All to keep the gravy train rolling in."

Shannon began to sob outright.

"Time to go," Teddy said. "Get up."

"You'd better go with him, Shannon," I said. She looked like a broken woman. Her head down, silent sobs wracking her narrow shoulders—

And then she launched herself at Teddy, windmilling her arms, slapping at his face, trying to claw him. It caught us all flatfooted. Teddy struggled to get Shannon under control. Too late, I started to make my move.

Way too late.

The man was already next to me with the muzzle of the gun just behind my ear. How he moved that fast, I had no idea. But any chance I had was gone.

Teddy finally pinned Shannon's arms against her sides and hauled her up the stairs. She was screaming at him and calling my name until he managed to clamp a hand over her mouth.

I heard her muffled sobs as she and Teddy stepped off the boat onto the dock.

The man and I stood there for a moment, the boat gently rocking from the departure of Teddy and Shannon.

I thought I was going to die. Ellen would probably find me. She'd have to call Anna. I wouldn't see my daughters grow up. For just a moment, I felt a sense of closure. The same man who had killed Benjamin Collins was now going to kill me.

"Just like old times," the man said, affecting an effeminate lilt to his voice. The same one that had fooled me a few years back. "Me and you," he said.

If I was going to die, I at least wanted some answers. I thought I deserved them before I had my brains splattered on the boat's walls.

"Who are you?" I asked.

He chuckled softly. There was a pause, and I expected to see a burst of light and then nothing but darkness.

Instead, the man said, "Start the boat."

Forty-five

There was now a raging storm on the water. Gray clouds obscured the stars, and white foam whipped off the waves.

With the man's gun trained on my head at all times, I backed the boat out of its slip, then pushed it toward the harbor opening where I could see Lake St. Clair in all its glorious frenzy. It had begun to rain, and the water came down in sheets, as if poured from the black sky. Chain lightning flashed on the horizon across the lake, over Canada.

I toyed with the idea of jumping overboard, but something told me I'd get as far as one step, maybe two, before my head was fully vented.

As I steered the *Air Fare*, I thought about how appropriate this was. The boy entrusted to me, Benjamin Collins, had been sliced up and found floating in Lake St. Clair. A lot of people blamed me, including myself, for what had happened. Although I hadn't actually been the one to kill him, I'd had the opportunity to save him, and I'd blown it.

So now here I was with his real killer, and I was faced with the same fate. I had a feeling I wasn't going to be able to save myself from him either. I could imagine the story in the newspaper: "Cop Killed in Same Manner as Earlier Victim." They'd have a field day with it. Or maybe the man here had a plan to make it look like a suicide. I was sure he had a plan.

"Where to?" I shouted as the rain whipped directly into my face.

"Out," he said.

Maybe he was going to conk me over the head and toss me overboard. Even in good shape, I'd have trouble swimming in this shit. Knocked unconscious, I wouldn't have a chance.

The *Air Fare* was a good-sized boat, twenty-nine-feet long. However, Lake St. Clair was some three hundred square miles, and waves commonly got as big as they do on Lake Huron, or even Lake Michigan. Right now, my boat was being tossed around pretty good. In fact, I'd never been out in water this rough. Wave after wave bashed into the prow, and we rode the water like a mechanical bull.

"Why?" I shouted to the man, who had now moved around directly behind me. He seemed a bit unsteady. If he killed me, how was he planning to get back to shore? Somehow, I was sure he would manage.

I glanced back at him, and he shook his head then gestured with the gun for me to look back to where I was going.

In my mind, some questions were starting to get answered. I'd always assumed that the man who'd killed Benjamin Collins had been a psychopath. Not a jilted lover. But now I knew for sure. My guess was that when I'd killed Erma and Freda, Teddy had brought in someone new. Or someone old, in this case.

The man was a hired killer.

So why had he killed Benjamin Collins? As soon as I thought about it, I realized it wasn't the right question.

"Who hired you to kill Benjamin Collins?"

I looked back, and he had a smirk on his face. He shook his head.

I turned back just as a giant wave washed over the front of the boat. Water hit me in the chest, and I staggered back. I didn't know what to be more afraid of. Being murdered by a contract killer. Or being washed overboard and drowning. Same result, different paths.

Did he plan on taking me over by the yacht club? Where he'd left the butchered body of Benjamin Collins? Right now, we were pointing straight out to the middle of the lake.

I heard the man singing behind me. Over the din of the wind and the rain and the crashing waves, this fucker was singing. I recognized the tune. "Let it Bleed" from the Rolling Stones. Wonderful.

It pissed me off. Here I was, about to die. My two daughters were about to lose their father, Anna was about to lose her husband, and my killer was singing. Having a grand old time. Well, fuck him.

I let go of the wheel and faced him. "You're the scum of the earth—just so you know," I shouted at him.

He continued his little musical number.

"You can kill me," I said. "But you're a coward. A rotten, murdering piece of dogshit."

The anger choked up inside me, and I realized there was no point in waiting. If I was going to die, I was going to die the way I wanted.

He seemed to read my mind.

He brought his gun up and now held it straight out from his body pointing at me.

"Come on, you rotten sonofabi—" I started to say.

A resounding crash screamed in my ears, and the boat's deck slipped out from underneath me. The splintering of wood shattered the sounds of the storm, and I landed on my side, pain slicing up my back. I saw the prow of another boat bisecting the *Air Fare*. Cut it right in fucking half.

The ship's prow was white, and I saw the line of blue down the side along with the word POLICE.

I struggled to get to my feet as water rushed all around me. The *Air Fare* was sagging, nearly broken in half.

A weight pressed on my back, and hands grasped the side of my head. My head was wrenched to the side, and the pain shot up my neck. He was on top of me, trying to break my neck. Unbelievable. How had he moved that fast? How had he gotten behind me again so soon after we were rammed?

Pain shot through my body, and I twisted beneath him. Just as I wondered why he wasn't shooting me, I realized he must have lost his gun.

I immediately stopped twisting and, instead, pulled him in the direction he was trying to make me go.

We both rolled and crashed against the side of the boat as another wave broke over us. It knocked him off me, and I thought I heard other voices shouting.

I got to my feet and whirled around just as he came at me. He hit me in the face and then in the stomach. My breath flew out of me in a gush, and then he whirled, a karate kick that would've finished the job of taking off my head had I not ducked at just the right moment. I slipped as another wave caught me full in the face, and my feet flew out from under me. I crashed into the *Air Fare*'s stern, which had become the receptacle for the damage done in the boat's middle.

I slumped to the deck, water up to my waist, and felt sharp fragments of wood scrape my back. I looked up and saw the impossible.

He was coming at me, full bore, with a steadiness and animal grace that made me look on in awe.

As I watched him come with the inevitability of Death itself, my hands wrapped around something that felt like a wooden bat. Just as he got close enough and I could see him winding up for another killer kick, I lashed out. The blow caught him in the side of the neck at just the right time. Off balance, he fell to the deck as another wave crashed over us. I was knocked down and the pole, which

I now saw was the jib's handle, had broken in half. A nasty, jagged break with a long sliver of wood jutting from the middle.

The Air Fare tilted, the weight of the water in the stern sending the bow up. The man slid down the deck toward me, blood in his mouth either from my blow or from being knocked down by a wave.

I raised the pole over my head with both hands and fell on top of him, driving the pole straight into him like a pile driver. My mind was on autopilot, just a raw, savage fury and a fear of dying pounding in my head.

I felt the pole plunge through his chest and bury itself in the softer wood of the deck. He reached for me, but I saw his eyes glaze. His arms went instead to the wooden spear, now rammed firmly into the sinking boat's deck. He tugged at it, but it didn't move.

Blood gushed from his mouth.

"Who are you?" I screamed at him. His eyes were open, and I thought he was going to speak.

Instead, he laughed.

There was another loud crack, but this time it wasn't thunder or another ship. It was the *Air Fare*. The boat seemed to break in half, and suddenly black water was below me and I was sinking. There was an explosion. A bright-orange flame licked the air, and I was under, trying to kick off my shoes and pants, my ribs and back and neck screaming in agony. I kicked toward the surface, my lungs on fire.

I broke through the surface only to have a wave slam into my face with such force that my head snapped back, and I saw black, and then green again as I was forced back underwater. I bobbed to the surface and heard voices. Something hit me in the face. It wasn't rain or wood debris from the boat.

It was rope.

I got my hands around it and felt myself being pulled. The blackness came again.

And this time, it stayed.

Forty-six

This is what it must be like to go insane. Black sky. Flashes of brilliant white. Ear-shattering cracks of thunder. A roaring motor. And the voices. The voices that shout your name. That shout nonsense. The voices that keep shouting long after you've tried to stop hearing them.

I went out, and when I came back, all I could tell was that everything felt soft. I felt a needle go in my arm.

And then more blackness.

•

"Laying around in bed," I heard a voice say. "How typical."

I struggled to open my eyes, but it was like jerking open an old garage door. The hinges felt rusty. The light that poured in was bright and stabbing. I closed my eyes again to try to stop the pain that seemed to pierce the middle of my head.

"Gross, look at how much he drooled on his pillow," the voice said again. This time I recognized the bemused irony.

"Ellen," I said. My throat felt like 60-grit sandpaper.
"Yeah?"
"Shut up," I managed.

"Oh, come on," she said. "I let you saw logs all night. I know how much you need your beauty sleep, but it's time to make your statement."

"I already did. I said shut up. That's my statement."

She sighed, and I heard the scrape of a chair across the floor. Now the voice was next to me. I opened my eyes, and she was handing me a glass with orange juice in it.

"Drink up, Gilligan," she said.

I took a drink and tried to sit up. My ribs ached, and I had a few thousand sore spots on my body. I took another drink and turned a small corner toward feeling human again.

"Start with when you left the scene of Molly's murder," she said.

It took me the better part of a half hour, with plenty of breaks, to describe the shootout with Erma and Freda, the connection I made between Rufus Coltraine and Memphis Bornais, and then my decision to meet Shannon on my boat.

When I got to the part about Teddy and his hired killer showing up, I said, "It was him, Ellen."

"Who?"

"The guy with Teddy. It was him. The guy who killed Benjamin Collins."

"Come again?" she said.

"I haven't lost my mind, Ellen."

"You need to rest," she said.

"No, I don't. It was him, Ellen. The guy I turned Benjamin Collins over to. The guy who cut him up and tossed him in the lake."

She held up her hands. "Okay, okay, let's finish talking about this later."

"But—"

"Shannon Sparrow showed up at the station this morning," Ellen said. "She has a little tape recorder she carries around for song ideas. She recorded her manager admitting to orchestrating the murders of Memphis and the others."

"And Teddy?"

She shook her head. "Gone."

That made sense to me. If he was connected, whether to the Mob or just the criminal underground in general, he'd probably have a way to hide. Who knew how much of Shannon's money he had squirreled away?

Ellen left then, and I retreated into my favorite hobby. Sleeping.

Forty-seven

People from across the border in Canada, people from Ohio, Indiana, and as far away as Chicago, began to show up as early as eight hours before the concert. Everyone was talking about the event on the radio. "Shannon Sparrow's free concert!" they boomed across the airwaves.

Coupled with the media attention the murders had created, Shannon's name had been splashed across the public's eye more times than could be counted. Some had even put forth a conspiracy theory that it was all a giant publicity stunt.

The show was being put on in the middle of the village. There were cop cars everywhere, roads had been blocked off, and the village was swarming with people.

I took Anna and the girls, and picked up Clarence Barre on the way. Shannon had given us all VIP passes so we could watch the concert from off to the side of the stage.

One of Shannon's roadies provided us with five chairs, and we sat down, at least the adults did. The girls were singing and dancing around, too keyed up to sit.

"Is this what your shows were like?" I asked Clarence.

"Yeah," he said. "I gave a lot of free shows too, but only because no one would pay me."

I had never really seen a happy Clarence before. Not that I would call him "happy," per se, but it did seem that a giant weight had been lifted from his shoulders. He'd taken the news well when I told him that a songwriter, Memphis Bornais, had arranged to have Jesse killed. And that, ultimately, Shannon's manager had tried to cover it all up.

He shook his head. It upset him that Jesse hadn't told him she was beginning to write songs. It made sense to me, from what I'd learned about her through Nevada Hornsby. Jesse was independent. She didn't want to tread on her father's name. And knowing that if she told him, he'd probably call up producers and performers he knew, using his contacts to give her a break, she had decided to go her own way.

"Gosh, they're beautiful," he said, gesturing toward my daughters. Isabel and Nina now had their arms around each other and were doing some kind of chorus line. Christ, what a couple of hams. Took after their mother obviously.

Anna put an arm around Clarence's shoulders.

"I'm glad John could help you," she said. "I can't imagine what you've been through, but I can guess that it feels good to have it resolved."

He nodded, his big, silvery mane flowing like expensive silk. Damn, Kenny Rogers was back.

A local disc jockey appeared on stage and did the usual big introduction for Shannon, and then amid thunderous applause and a few pyrotechnics, she appeared.

Shannon wore a short skirt, cowboy boots, and a white blouse. I recognized her band mates even though most of them now looked sober. I'd only seen them when they were drunk or getting stoned.

Anna, Clarence, and I all applauded.

Shannon slung the guitar over her shoulders.

It was a beautiful instrument, handmade by Jesse Barre. The cops eventually found it at Memphis Bornais' farmhouse, in her music room. On public display. The cops actually gave it to Clarence, but he felt that it was intended all along for Shannon, so it was hers now.

Shannon stepped to the microphone.

"I'd like to dedicate this concert to a very special person," Shannon said. "Her name is Jesse Barre. She had beauty inside her. And she created beauty in everything she did."

I stole a glance at Clarence. He was already starting to cry.

"She made this guitar," Shannon said, and she lifted it off her chest away from her body, toward the crowd. It truly looked spectacular under the lights. The very embodiment of beauty.

"She also had just begun to write songs, before her life was tragically taken from her."

Clarence stood, and Shannon looked at him.

"I'm going to record her songs and put out a CD next year," Shannon said. "The proceeds of which will go to the Jesse Barre Foundation."

The crowd applauded. I admired Shannon. She was trying to do the right thing.

"Here's a little something she wrote. I don't know for sure if she had her father in mind when she wrote it, but I have a feeling she did."

Shannon put the pick to the strings, and the song seemed to flow out of her. I thought of all the tragedy, the killing and lives wasted over the music I was hearing now.

I hugged Anna.

I hugged the girls

And I even hugged Clarence.

Shannon was right.

Jesse Barre created beauty.

I was seeing it right now.

Forty-eight

Ellen was in a meeting with a task force from Wayne
County, which was formed to track down a prostitution
ring believed to be bringing in teenage girls against their
will from cities like Chicago and Cleveland.

I sat in Ellen's office, listening to the cop chatter in
the hallways, the traffic out on Mack Avenue.

For the first time in my life, I felt hope. Hope that one
day I might catch the man who killed Benjamin Collins.
They say that you never know what life will bring you.
That what initially appears to be great misfortune can
often turn into great opportunities.

When Teddy Armbruster showed up on my boat, I
thought it was all over.

Now, I realized, it was a new beginning.

•

"Haven't you given me enough paperwork to deal
with?" Ellen said, breezing into her office, the leather of
her gun belt creaking like an old saddle.

"Hey, I'm just another taxpayer making sure I get my
money's worth. Public servants like you need to be kept to
task, my dear," I said.

"God, you're such an ass," she said.

"I want the Benjamin Collins file."

She laughed outright. "Oh sure. A private citizen demanding police files—open cases, at that. What next? You want a shotgun? Borrow a squad car? Take a couple Kevlar vests for the kids?"

"The case is open?" I asked.

"Did I say that?" she said.

"Yeah, you did."

"Well, I guess it is, then."

"Had it been moved from the cold case files?"

She didn't answer that right away.

"Come on, Ellen . . . it's me, John. Your brother."

This softened her just a bit, although she still didn't say anything.

"Has Teddy started talking?" I asked.

Armbruster was busted in Chicago, trying to go undercover with his Mob friends, but he got caught on an FBI surveillance camera going into a house. He was brought back to Detroit the day before.

She shook her head. "He's dummied up with the best Mob defense lawyer money can buy."

"It'll be a long trial," I said.

She nodded.

I took a deep breath.

"I need that file, Ellen."

"What are you going to do with it?"

I knew what she meant, but instead, I said "Go to Kinko's and copy it . . . have it back on your desk in fifteen minutes. No one the wiser."

She looked at me, really studying me. "Are you going to do anything stupid?"

"Of course I am. That's my whole modus operandi."

"I know, but something that will get you killed and leave Anna and those girls without a father?"

I shook my head. "Absolutely not. But now that I know Benjamin Collins was most likely a hit—a contract kill—that changes everything."

She sighed and pulled the file out of one of her desk drawers. I knew she didn't usually keep files there, so she'd had it ready for me. This was all a pretense—a warning to take it easy and take it slow.

I would do my best.

I took the file and said, "I'll be back in fifteen minutes."

"Don't bother," she said. "That's a copy."

She smiled at that.

"Thanks," I said.

"Just trying to keep the taxpayers happy," she said.

Forty-nine

It had all started with the lake.

I pulled my car off Lake Shore Drive, parked it on an opposing street, and walked down to the water's edge.

It was a calm morning, the lake a sheet of blue-green glass. I had the file in my hand, and I sat down on the grass. The grass was cold and damp, but somehow everything felt good and felt right.

I felt like I belonged here.

They never found the man's body. The next day, divers had gone down to my boat, which had broken up into a few hundred pieces. They found lots of debris: wood, pieces of the radio, and minutia from the boat's cabin.

But they didn't find a body.

I knew there was no way he could have survived being impaled and then taken underwater. He would have had to somehow swim to shore with a devastating injury in the middle of five-foot waves.

Impossible.

It didn't matter to me, though.

He was alive now in my memory. And dead or alive, I knew he would lead me to the final answer as to what happened to Benjamin Collins.

That's really all that mattered.

I looked at the file in my lap. This was going to be my chance to set things right. Redemption, I guess.

I took a deep sigh and ran my finger along the inside of the file's cover.

I held my breath.

And opened the file.

THE END

About the Author

Dan Ames is an internationally best selling crime novelist and winner of the Independent Book Award for Crime Fiction. You can learn more about him at AuthorDanAmes.com

Made in the USA
Middletown, DE
06 June 2019